A Wizard
Called Jones

Clare Cooper

Pont Books

First published by Hodder and Stoughton 1984
New edition by Pont Books, Gomer Press 1994

ISBN 1 85902 075 5

This volume is published with the support of the Welsh Arts Council.

Printed by
J.D. Lewis & Sons Ltd., Gomer Press, Llandysul, Dyfed

Preface

Simon Jones had always thought of himself as an ordinary boy with below average sight and more than average interest in mathematics and insects. But then he went to live on a mountain on the west coast of Wales, and he discovered that he wasn't ordinary at all.

He met a girl called Fred who took him home with her to her Aunt Meryl's house, Tŷ Corn Du . . . The house of the Black Horn. The black horn was a unicorn's horn which hung in the hall of the house, and Simon discovered that, when he held the black horn in his hands, he could make magic. He also discovered that he had Second Sight.

He didn't like being strange like this, but Aunt Meryl's Chinese friend, Mr Smith, convinced him that he shouldn't worry about it, and Fred told him about a wonderful wizard who had once lived at Tŷ Corn Du, and about a legend which said that, one day, a new wizard would come to live there.

When Simon was able to use the black horn to rescue a unicorn which the first wizard had left hidden on the mountain, Fred was convinced that Simon was that new wizard. Simon, however, was not so sure, and is still not sure when this story begins.

1
Golden Bees

Simon sat in the school bus thinking about magic. He usually thought about magic as he sat there, looking over the hedges and across the fields for the first glimpse of the mountain. But, today, as well as the wonderful mountain, he was thinking about the unicorn's horn which hung on the wall in the hall of Tŷ Corn Du, the old house where his friend, Fred, lived with her Aunt Meryl and her Uncle Smithy.

It seemed to Simon that he and Fred had spent most of the last holiday arguing about the unicorn's horn. Fred wanted him to take it and keep it with him on the mountain, but he didn't want to. It had belonged at Tŷ Corn Du for hundreds of years, and he thought that it should stay there. 'I'll borrow it one day, if I need it,' he told her, 'but I don't need it yet.'

He sighed. 'She'll be going back to school next week,' he thought. 'It would be nice if we could stop arguing about it before she goes. Perhaps if she comes over this evening I'll manage to make her understand how I feel about it. I'll have a really good try, anyway . . . if she comes.'

Usually, Fred rode across the estuary to Simon's house every evening, but at the moment she had what she called 'a single parent problem'. Fred's mother had gone away and left her when she was very young. She still had a father, but she didn't see him very often, except when he came for short, weekend visits, which, usually, she loved. But, this holiday, he had already stayed for a week, and hadn't said anything about when he planned to go back to London ... and everyone at Tŷ Corn Du wished that he *would* go back.

Simon knew that Fred felt very guilty about wishing this. 'Usually I love him being here,' she had told him. 'Guy's great, he really is, Jonesy, and this long stay should be a treat for me ... but it isn't. He's such a misery this time. I dread being on my own with him. I really do.'

'I hope she can come over,' Simon thought. 'It cheers her up to come over and chat to Mother. And if she comes tonight I'll take her right up to the carn. She likes it up there nearly as much as I do.'

The bus stopped with a jolt at the crossroads in the village, and Simon joined the pushing, shoving horde eager to get off. There were shouts of 'See ya, Jonesy!' and 'Bye Simon!'

'See ya!' he shouted back, and set off along the road towards the lane which led, up the lower slopes of the mountain, to his house, Tŷ Corn Du Bach.

Simon loved walking along the lane. He swung his school bag on to his shoulder, straightened his back, and breathed in deeply. The mountain always felt so wonderful. He looked up at the very top, at the carn. He couldn't see it properly. His eyes weren't good enough for that. But he could imagine it perfectly. He knew, by heart, every grey, lichen-covered stone in the carn. 'Yes,' he thought. 'If Fred comes over we'll go for a walk up there.'

About half-way along the lane, red dead nettles had overgrown the ditch. They had been beautiful all through July and August. Deep red spikes had thrust upward from a tracery of leaves, filling the ditch with colour. Now, in early September, they were past their best. The red spikes had turned into dry, brown husks, filled with shining black seeds, ready to be shaken, like grains of pepper, all over the banks and verges. But there were still some red flowers left, and it was still a favourite place for bees.

All summer Simon had watched bees there. He liked bees. They were tawny bumble bees, covered with hair, robust creatures, always busy. He stopped now, and bent down, peering closely at the drying flowers.

Suddenly, a bee came. It flew, darting, close to his face. He jerked away. 'That's not tawny! That's golden! It's one of that golden sort.'

He stood up and listened. Was it still there? . . . He couldn't hear it. It had gone. No, it hadn't. There it was again! He stood quite still and watched the small, gleaming insect as it flew close to his face. 'I wish I knew what sort they are,' he thought. He couldn't find these golden bees in any of his insect books, and no one he had asked had been able to tell him what they were.

The bee flew away, darting suddenly over his shoulder, down the lane, towards the estuary.

Whenever he saw one of these golden bees it went that way. He hadn't seen many of them, just the odd one, now and then, here in the lane, never anywhere else, and it always darted away towards the estuary. Before it went it always seemed to fly close to him for a moment, as though it was looking at him . . . he was almost sure that every one of those bees had looked at him.

He walked forward a few steps . . . another bee came. 'Two in one day!' Simon was surprised. He stood still again and tried to look at this one properly as it flew slowly beside him. It was completely golden. Its body seemed to have been forged of thinly-beaten gold-plate. Its legs were golden too, and covered with fine, golden hairs. Even its eyes were golden, and its wings were a hazy, golden blur. He wished that he could see one of these bees settled on the red dead nettles. Motionless those wings must be beautiful.

This bee darted away too, and Simon realized that, as he watched it, he had held his breath. Now he relaxed again and breathed in deeply. 'It *was* watching me,' he thought. 'It definitely was, and so was the other one. They all do, definitely.' Somehow, it made him feel uneasy.

Until then, when he had only suspected that these bees looked at him, he had been pleased. He had watched insects all his life, it seemed, and now he had found an insect that watched him. There had been a kind of satisfying justice in the situation. But, until then, he had only seen one, or maybe two, of them watching him in perhaps a whole week, or even a month. Now, today, he had been watched by two of them in what could have been only one minute.

Suddenly another one came. This one startled him. It came so close that he thought it would settle on his glasses. He didn't like that at all. But this one flew over his shoulder, too, darting quickly. Next moment another one was there. Simon almost swatted this one. He stopped himself, and dodged it instead, jerking his head aside out of its path. He began to hurry. This wasn't fun. Another one came, and another . . . Simon began to run.

And instantly bees came from nowhere. From nowhere and everywhere they came. Golden bees, hundreds of golden bees. Around him they whirled, around and around, and then up, up high into the air. Simon looked up. They hung above him, a golden cloud. For one moment they hung . . . and then they dropped.

He half screamed. He shut his eyes and threw up his arms to shield his face. He felt a warm breeze in his hair. The breeze of hundreds of golden wings. At any moment he would feel their feet, hundreds of prickling, clawing feet . . . and they might sting!

He screamed again, but his arms muffled the sound and turned it to a choke. He could feel the breeze of their wings, and smell their honey scent, and hear their hum, a low, loud throbbing hum, a sound like the purr of a tiger. But they didn't sting him. They didn't even touch him.

Very cautiously, he opened his eyes, and moved his arms until he could just see between them. Bees flew all around him, circling him in a tightly-packed, golden band. They might sound like a tiger, but they looked like a serpent, a coiling, twisting, golden serpent.

And although this serpent of bees kept well away from him, Simon knew that it had caught him. He knew that he couldn't move. He had to stay there, captive.

2

Bethan and Gareth

> '*Bees of gold*
> *Bright and bold*
> *All is told . . .*'

Simon listened. Someone was chanting. Someone, somewhere outside the serpent of bees. '*Away!*' he heard, and, instantly, the whole, golden animal vanished.

13

He stood there, still too afraid to move. In front of him a girl a little younger than he was and a very small boy stood staring at him. The boy was thin and very fair. The girl was a little more solid-looking and dark. At first, they both looked as frightened as he did, but, gradually, a critical look came into the boy's brown eyes, and he sounded almost scornful when he spoke.

'That's never him!' he said.

'It must be,' the girl told him. 'Her bees had found him on the mountain, she said. They would show us who he was, she said. Her bees wouldn't make a mistake, she said.'

'No, they wouldn't an' all, would they.' The boy sighed. 'He's not much to look at, though, is he, Bethan? I thought he'd look special.'

'He wouldn't look like the pictures of wizards in books, she said.'

All this time, ever since the bees had begun to circle him, Simon had been trying to stay calm. He knew that this had to be something magic happening to him. But he told himself that it was all right. He had coped with magic before. He could cope with it now. 'It's all right! I mustn't panic,' he told himself. But when he heard the girl say the word 'wizard', he did panic. These two were looking for a wizard, and they had found *him*.

'I'm not a wizard,' he said quickly. 'The bees must have made a mistake.'

'Never!' The girl shook her head. 'Old Blodwen's bees don't make mistakes. You've got to be the wizard.'

'Yes, you've got to be the wizard,' the boy echoed her. 'You do *know* that you're a wizard, don't you? You're only saying that you aren't, aren't you?' he asked.

'Course he's only saying that he isn't!' The girl shook him by the hand that she was holding tightly. 'He's not bigheaded about it, see.' She looked at Simon. 'Old Blodwen said you'd have Second Sight. Have you?'

'W-well,' Simon began to stutter. 'I c-can some-times s-see things.'

'And she said you'd got a unicorn's horn that you could do things with. Have you?'

'W-well, yes . . . well, but . . . '

'There, Gareth! He's the wizard all right,' the girl said, shaking the little boy again. 'I knew he had to be.'

The boy pulled his hand away from hers. 'I never said he wasn't.' He looked Simon up and down. 'He still looks scared after them bees,' he said.

'Course he does!' The girl looked concerned. 'You look as though you could do with a nice cup of tea,' she said to Simon. 'How about taking us home with you, eh? We could do with a cuppa too, to be quite honest with you. Been waiting for you all day, we have. Do you think . . .?' She smiled shyly. 'I don't like to cadge tea, not from a stranger, but you'll be glad to be sitting down with a cup of tea inside you when you hear what we've got to tell you, believe you me.'

It was like a nightmare. Simon could hardly believe that it was happening. They walked, one on his left, one on his right, as though they were making sure that he couldn't run away. He felt like a prisoner being escorted to some dark cell. But all they were doing was walking home to tea with him. He noticed that the boy kept looking over his shoulder. He glanced back too. A tall, golden column of bees stood in the lane. There was no escape that way either.

'I should have guessed that those bees were *different* when I couldn't find them in a book,' he thought. 'I should have done something about them. But what? What could I have done? I don't know how to *do* magic. My magic always just seems to sort of happen on its own. I don't know how to do it on purpose.' He wanted to run, to fly away, to vanish . . . but he couldn't. He could do nothing but take these two complete strangers home with him, and listen to what they had to say. 'But it's no use even listening,' he thought desperately. 'They want a wizard, and I don't know how to be a wizard.'

He felt better while they were indoors with Mother. She made everything instantly normal. She thought that Bethan and Gareth were two friends he had brought home from the school bus, and made fresh orange-juice for them all, and put it on a tray with three large chunks of fruit cake.

'Take it into the garden,' she said. 'Dad has left a boat plan spread out on the dining-room table, and I've got garden plans all over the kitchen.' The house was a glorious, normal muddle. But, as they sat on the steps in the middle of the rockery, immediately, the feeling of nightmare muddle began again.

Two golden bees crawled from beneath the collar of Bethan's shirt and settled on her shoulder. Only a few minutes before, Simon had been wishing that he could see one of them with its wings still, but, now that he could, he dared not look. These two bees were watching him. They were listening. He took a gulp of his mother's orange-juice and looked away, up at the carn, high above him. Looking at the carn was comforting. When he turned back to Bethan and Gareth afterwards, he even managed to sound confident.

'Well, perhaps you could begin by telling me who told you to come and find me,' he suggested.

'Miss Blodwen Emmanuel told us,' Bethan said.

'Who's she?'

'She's a witch,' Gareth said at once.

'She's an old lady who knows everything,' Bethan corrected him. 'You know we said it's best not to call her *that* . . . just in case.'

'Just in case what?' Simon asked.

'In case *they* tell her and she don't like it,' Gareth said, glancing warily at the bees on Bethan's shoulder. 'They get you, if she don't like you.'

Simon interrupted quickly. Gareth was making him feel almost panic-stricken. 'All right!' he said firmly as he could. 'Someone called Miss Blodwen Emmanuel sent you to find me, Is that right?'

'Yes. At least, her bees found you, and she sent us to tell you,' Bethan told him.

'And to tell you that you must help us, and that you've got to come and see her right away,' Gareth said.

Simon began to panic again. 'But I can't help. I really can't, you know, and, anyway, I'm back at school. I've got homework.'

'But Miss Emmanuel says that you're the only one who *can* help.' Gareth sounded frantic. 'She won't. And if you can't, what are we going to do?'

'Shut up, Gareth, for goodness sake. He will help,' Bethan said. She looked at Simon. 'You will, you know. You'll have to, if she says you must . . . Gareth's right about the bees, see.'

Gareth still looked terrified. 'Yes! She does set them on people. I said she does. You'll have to do everything she wants. She'll help you. She will. I'm sure. But she says she won't do it herself.'

'Do what?' Simon asked. He had suddenly realized that he had no idea what this terrible panic was about. 'Exactly what does she say I've got to do?'

Gareth looked at Bethan. 'Bethan's got to tell you all of it,' he said. Suddenly he looked as though he was afraid of Simon. 'Miss Emmanuel said you would be mad—as mad as she is—but you won't be, will you, even though you are a wizard?'

'Gareth!' Bethan sounded exasperated. '*He* won't be mad at us. Shut up being scared, will you!' She turned to face Simon. 'I think you're going to be more worried than mad,' she said, and took a deep breath. 'Two days ago,' she told him, 'me and Gareth were playing after school in an old barn on a farm near where we live. We were playing hide and seek, and Gareth thought he would hide up high in the roof, so he climbed right up on to a huge, great beam —and found a bottle there.'

'Yes!' Gareth interrupted her. 'Hidden in a sort of cut out place, it was, all secret.'

'Yes!' Bethan said firmly, and he sat quietly again. 'Well, it had a roll of old, dried-up paper stuck inside

19

it, so he brought it down to show me, and we got the paper out and unrolled it, and it had a poem written on it—at least, it was a sort of poem. It was funny. I couldn't read it at all, to begin with. The words were nearly all ones I'd never seen before, and Gareth didn't know any of them, of course. Well, *he* wasn't really interested by now, anyway, but I kept on trying to get them right. I kept on trying different ways of saying them as we went back home. Oh, I should have told you, we were on that path where there's a wishing well. Do you know it?'

'Yes.' Simon did. It was one of Fred's short cuts.

Bethan went on. 'It was funny, but just as I got to the wishing well, all the words made sense. I sort of stood there and read them to myself first—and then I shouted the whole poem out loud to Gareth. He was marching on ahead, see. And then, all of a sudden, this huge, grey dog was there. Drinking at the well, he was.' She looked at Simon seriously. 'He appeared. You know, the opposite to vanished. He appeared, and he seemed to think that I'd called him.' As she remembered it all Bethan began to look frightened. 'He came right up to me—right up close —and ever since then he's been following me. Every-where I go, he follows me.' She stopped talking and began to chew her lip. She looked as though she was going to cry.

'That's not the worst bit,' Gareth said. 'I'll tell you

the worst bit. Yesterday,' he told Simon, 'when we was walking past Miss Emmanuel's, she sent the bees out to stop us, just like they stopped you, only it was worse for us 'cause Miss Emmanuel came rushing out too, screaming at us.'

Bethan managed to join in again. 'It was awful,' she said. 'Mam's always telling us not to aggravate her, and we didn't know we had, but there she was screaming at us. "What are you doing with that dog?" she screeched. "Don't you know who it is you've got there?"'

'She was horr-' Gareth looked quickly at the bees. 'She was ever so cross. And she was crosser still when Bethan said we didn't know what she was going on about. "That's Cafall, you've got there," she screamed, and when we said: "Who's Cafall?" she made the bees whizz all over the place. "He's Arthur's dog!" she shouted at us. "He's Arthur's great, royal hound."'

'Who's Arthur?' Simon asked.

'*You know*!' Bethan said. 'Arthur of the Britons whom some people do call King.'

Simon stared at her. He wanted to say: 'But that's impossible,' to laugh, and say that it must be a joke, but because of all the things that had happened to him since he came to live on the mountain, he knew that it wasn't impossible. He knew that Miss

Emmanuel, whoever she was, was very probably right. 'Is she sure?' was all he could say to Bethan.

'Yes,' Bethan said. 'The bees told her, and they're always right. And, anyway, the dog comes when you call him.' She looked really frightened. 'He'll be somewhere near. He's always somewhere near—I suppose you ought to see him, didn't you,' she said, and then, looking as though she would rather be doing anything else in the world, Bethan stood up and called.

'Cafall, Cafall!' she called, and it sounded almost like a song. 'Cafall, Cafall!'

The mountain seemed to lie still in the moment that followed the sound of the great hound's name. Even the sea seemed to whisper and ebb far, far away.

Simon stood up. Was Cafall really there? Arthur's Cafall? Would he come when this girl called his name? Simon waited . . .

And suddenly, without warning, Cafall came. Over the high, stone wall he came in one, great leap. Then he stood there, among the late roses, his head held high, his red tongue lolling, his teeth glistening like ivory in his mighty jaws. Cafall was huge. Cafall was powerful. And the gleam in his eyes was fierce and wild. Cafall was not tame. He was not a pet dog, not the sort of dog that lies on sofas and basks in front of fires. Cafall was a hunting dog, a dog which knew how to chase, how to fight—and, most certainly, Cafall knew how to kill.

3
Fred in Charge

Cafall soon left the garden again. He looked suspiciously at Simon, and seemed to satisfy himself that
Bethan was there, then leapt back over the wall and
disappeared.

'He's gone!' Simon said, and realized that he was
shaking. He sat down quickly, and clutched at his
reassuringly normal glass of orange-juice.

'He hasn't really gone,' Bethan said. 'He's still
there, somewhere. He lurks, see. We don't see him
very often, but he's there. He . . . he follows me.
Even to school, he follows me. Miss Emmanuel says
he's expecting me to take him back to his home, back
to Arthur, and I shouldn't never have meddled with
an old spell if I didn't know how to undo it. But how
was I to know it was a spell?' She was trying desperately not to cry. 'It's all so awful. He's a horrible dog,
but I feel so sorry for him. What if I've taken him
away from his home for ever—taken him away from
his master, from Arthur? I feel so mean about what
I've done to him. But I'm frightened of him too—
Terrified! He's not a pet, see.'

'I did see,' Simon said.

'He's got scars all over him,' Gareth said. 'When he

comes up close you can see them. He's got bite marks all over his legs from where he's been fighting wolves, and a long, thin, purple line right between his eyes, as though he's been cut with a sword—as though he's been fighting a battle at Arthur's side.' Gareth sounded excited.

Simon wished that he could feel excited. But he couldn't. All he could feel was frightened. It was awful—and they expected him to put it right. They expected him to get rid of this great beast of a dog. And he had no idea what to do.

He was just beginning another terrible moment of panic when he heard Fred coming along the lane. He heard the donkey, Gwenhwyfar's hooves first, as they clinked against the stones half buried in the dry mud, and then he heard Fred's dog begin to bark.

'Bedwyr!' he said, and now he did panic. 'Cafall could kill him.'

They all rushed to the wall and scrambled to lean over it. Bedwyr was scuttling to catch up with Fred, his tail pressed firmly between his legs, and Fred was looking at Bethan and Gareth with excitement and envy in her eyes.

Fred knew Bethan and Gareth. 'Hello!' she said. 'What are you two doing here? Brass bedknobs! Don't say that fabulous wolfhound is yours!'

'A fabulous wolfhound,' Simon thought. 'That's

exactly what Cafall is. Trust Fred to get it right without even knowing that she has.'

Bethan was shy of Fred. 'He's not ours, really,' she said. 'At least, I suppose he is, sort of, mine for the moment, but only sort of.'

'You'd better come in and sit down while they explain,' Simon said.

Of course, when Fred heard the story, she was thrilled. 'Brass bedknobs!' she said again. 'Fancy Cafall coming back! Fancy Cafall, and not Arthur. It's supposed to be Arthur who'll come back, isn't it, but here you are with Cafall instead. I can hardly believe it.'

'You make it sound exciting when you say it like that,' Bethan said, and glanced at Simon. 'I can't say I'm thrilled, though—and nor is *he*.'

Fred ignored her. 'And fancy that old crosspatch, Blodwen Emmanuel, being a real witch. I never thought she was a real one. She used to tell fortunes at fetes and that, didn't she, before she got so very old. Do you remember how she used to sit in a dark tent, all wrapped up in a black shawl. I suppose you two knew she was real, living down there so close to her, but I never even guessed. But I never knew she kept bees, either. They're not the sort of thing I notice, as a rule, except when I'm out with you Jonesy. Well, you'll have to go and see her, and right away, too.'

'But I've got homework . . .'

'Oh, Jonesy! Homework! Trust you to be bothered about something as ordinary as homework at a time like this. I know a good short cut to Blodwen's. We'll have to be back pretty quickly, or I will, anyway. Guy's taking me out for a meal again.' Fred looked gloomy. 'He's more miserable than ever . . . but let's not talk about that. Let's try to work out what you'll have to do. You'll have to come and fetch the horn from my place, of course. You'll need the horn.'

Simon began to feel confused. Fred was rushing him, as usual. 'I might not need the horn,' he said.

'Of course you will!' Fred looked annoyed with him. 'Blodwen told them you had a unicorn's horn, didn't she? Of course you'll need it. It'll show that you're The Wizard of the Black Horn, even if you don't have to use it. Come on, now!'

Fred soon had them all hurrying along the lane towards the path she knew which would take them quickly, to Miss Emmanuel's cottage. She began to tell Bethan and Gareth about the black horn, and how Simon had used it once before. 'Of course,' Simon heard her say, 'Jonesy isn't the first Wizard of the Black Horn, you know. There was another one once, but he lived where my Aunt Meryl's house is now. He was fantastically powerful, as good as Myrddin, even. Jonesy's going to be just as good, one day.'

Simon kept behind them all. He walked along with Bedwyr panting at his side. He wished that Fred wouldn't rush him. He would have liked more time to think. He would have liked time to look up Cafall in a book. He needed time to find out how to get rid of him. He had no idea how to get rid of him. What had Miss Emmanuel said . . . that Cafall had to be sent back to where he had come from? But where had he come from?

Suddenly, Simon noticed that Bedwyr was whimpering quietly. He looked down at him. Bedwyr's tail was pressed between his legs again. He was looking back along the path. Simon glanced back too, half expecting to see the column of bees again. But it wasn't bees. It was Cafall.

With head held low, now, tongue lolling thirstily, and dark eyes staring beneath thick, grey brows, Cafall loped silently after them.

He was terrifying. He was more terrifying than Simon had imagined. Now he knew exactly why Bethan couldn't feel thrilled.

'I can't deal with this.' Simon turned away from Cafall and stared straight ahead, afraid to glance back again. 'They need a real wizard to deal with this.' He stumbled along, terribly aware of being the last one in the line of people on the path. 'I don't know what to do. I don't know what to do. Cafall could walk around like this for ever. He could haunt the town. He could haunt the mountain—for ever. Somebody must help me. This Miss Emmanuel. Yes, this Miss Emmanuel *must* help.'

4

The Caravanners . . . and Miss Emmanuel

Cafall followed them until they reached the lane that ran along beside the caravan park. The last time Simon had walked that way with Fred it had been a noisy, bustling, overcrowded place, alive with radios and laughing, shouting people. Now, it was half empty. In fact, they only saw two people.

One of these was Bethan and Gareth's mother. She came to the door of the site office as they passed, and waved and shouted to them that tea was ready. Gareth wanted to go in right away, but Bethan wouldn't let him.

'You'd best come right to Old Blodwen's, Gareth,' she said. 'We must both come back with the wizard, she said. We'd best not aggravate her.' She called to her mother. 'We won't be long, Mam.' Her mother waved again, and went indoors.

All they saw of the other person on the site was a small, pale face at the window of the caravan next to the office. It looked out, saw them on the path, and dodged back in quickly.

'Hello!' Fred said. 'You haven't still got people staying here, have you?'

'Only two,' Bethan said. 'That one's Poor Miriam.'

'Why *poor* Miriam?' Fred wanted to know. 'Is she hard up?'

'No, not that sort of poor. At least, we don't think so. Poor miserable, that's what I meant.'

Fred sighed. 'Like my father. Poor Guy. He's terribly miserable at the moment.'

'What's the matter with him?'

'I don't know!' Fred wailed. 'I'm doing my best to cheer him up. Brass bedknobs! I'm doing everything I can think of to cheer him up—and so I should, too, as I'm his nearest and dearest. I only hope Poor Miriam's nearest and dearest have better results with her than I do with Guy. What's the matter with her, I wonder.'

'I think she's crossed in love,' Bethan said.

Gareth made a rude noise. 'You're *twp*, you are, Bethan Rhys. She's just fed up 'cause she stays stuck in that caravan waitin' for company half the time, Tad says. She's not crossed in love,' he said scornfully.

'Mam thinks she is, then! Mam says she goes out to meet somebody secretly. Always slipping off all on her own, she is.'

'So's Dr Gimlett, too, but you'd never say she was crossed in love.'

'Who's Dr Gimlett?' Fred asked.

The question had an unexpected effect. Instantly, Bethan and Gareth both looked extremely annoyed.

'She's an old fuss-pot,' Gareth said.

'She's a bossy, old, stupid know-all.' Bethan went quite red with irritation at the very thought of Dr Gimlett. 'She's the worst one we've had on the site all summer,' she said. 'Nothing's right. She's nosy. She tries to tell Tad how to run the place. She knows everything. Ugh! Go on about Dr Gimlett all day, I could.'

'Me and Tad runs away from her,' Gareth told them, sniggering behind his hand.

'You can laugh!' Bethan said to him. 'Me and Mam can't. Somebody's got to be polite, after all, or the place might get a bad name. Do you know,' she told Fred, 'she makes Mam cook an evening meal specially for her. The restaurant's shut now, but Dr Gimlett can't even boil an egg proper, so poor old Mam's cooking specially for her every night.'

'Go on!' Fred said. 'I didn't know your caravan people could be that bad.'

'Well, they're not as a rule. Dr Gimlett's something apart, she is!' Bethan said, and then she and Fred began to complain happily about the trials of being invaded by tourists every holiday.

31

It was all so normal, just like an ordinary walk in a quiet lane in late summer. Simon began to wonder if, perhaps, he had imagined that it was all so terrible. But, as he stepped on to the narrow path that led away from the lane, towards Miss Emmanuel's cottage, he felt the nightmare clutch at him more desperately than ever. Tall trees cast suffocating shadows, and a cliff-like slope rose in darkness at one side. He was shut in. He was trapped. They were making him walk into the most narrow valley he had ever seen, with the cliff on one side, and a dark, swiftly-flowing river on the other. And somewhere at the end of it a cantankerous, old woman who expected him to make magic. 'At least I'm not on my own,' he thought. 'At least Fred's here.'

But he was on his own.

Miss Emmanuel stood waiting for them just inside her garden gate. As Gareth ran up, she stepped out of the shadow of her tall hedge, and put her hand on the latch before he could lift it and let them in. Simon couldn't see her properly, but he did see Gareth step back and put his hands in his pockets quickly, as though he had never intended to open the gate anyway. He also heard her voice. It was a harsh voice, low and grating, with just the hint of a whine in it—an unpleasant voice.

'That'll do!' She spoke to Bethan and Gareth. 'Done your bit, you have. Now go on home—and

look after that dog. You'll have forgotten all about looking after him, poor brute, no doubt. Go on home, and don't forget he's your responsibility, until I say he's not.'

Gareth turned away at once, but Bethan hesitated.

'I said, off you go!' Miss Emmanuel raised her hand and pointed at her. Bethan went.

Then it was Fred's turn. Miss Emmanuel peered up at her as she sat looking down from Gwenhwyfar's back. There was a definite whine in her voice as she spoke to Fred. 'Well, it's Miss Frederika of Tŷ Corn Du,' she whimpered. 'I haven't seen you since I had to give up my feting and all that caper. What a fine, big girl you are now! Indeed yes! And it's pleased I am to have you here, though not surprised . . . But it's not you I have to see Miss Frederika, so off you go now, like a good girl, and remember me to your aunty, Miss Meryl . . . and her new Chinaman husband, too, if you please.' She waited, pointedly, for Fred to go, tapping her foot impatiently.

Fred hesitated too. She looked at Simon and then at the old woman, and then back at Simon. 'I'll have to go,' she said apologetically.

Simon tried to say: 'It's all right,' but his voice seemed to have disappeared. He cleared his throat.

'See you tomorrow,' Fred said to him. 'Be sure to come to my place. I'll be expecting you.' She wheeled Gwenhwyfar. 'Goodnight, Miss Emmanuel,' she said, and then she moved away quickly. All too soon, as Simon watched her go, she was nothing but a white blur in the shadows of the trees. He was left alone, with Miss Emmanuel.

5

Simon and Miss Emmanuel

'In you come, Corn Du,' Miss Emmanuel said. 'In you come.' The gate clicked as she opened it, and clicked again more loudly as she shut it behind him.

It was as he followed her along her winding garden path that Simon saw she was covered with golden bees. They clung to her long, brown skirt, and crawled over her honey-coloured blouse. And her hair . . . her hair was yellow with pollen. Simon stared appalled. Miss Emmanuel's hair was a nest of bees! They wove in and out of it, in and out and to and fro, sometimes dropping to her shoulders, sometimes flying up to circle her head before settling back again. And everywhere, the air was filled with humming, the quiet humming of self-satisfied bees.

'It's pleased we are that you've come, me and my bees,' Miss Emmanuel told him, as she opened her front door. 'In you go,' she said and stood aside as Simon lowered his head slightly and stepped down one deep step into her cottage. Then she stepped in behind him and bolted the door.

Simon looked around, and immediately saw that the room that he had stepped into was beautiful. He was surprised. He had expected it to be dark and dirty, and untidy too, but it wasn't. It was light and clean and beautiful. But there was something strange about it.

He sat where Miss Emmanuel told him to sit while she made tea, and looked around, trying to decide what, exactly, was strange. The room was full of colour. That was why it looked beautiful. There were rugs and cushions and shawls everywhere—and flowers. The room was filled with flowers. And it was so light! But it shouldn't be light. That was what was strange. He looked at the locked door, at the one, small window. Not much light could come in that way. And there was no lamp, no candle, nothing —except the fire.

All of the light in the room came from the fire. It was a strange fire, strange and frightening, for, when he tried to look at it he couldn't. The flames hurt his eyes. Whenever he tried to see them, he was forced to turn away. All he could do was look at the fire's reflection in the copper plates on the dresser. It glowed, a complete fire, in every one of them. It twinkled in the cut-glass tumblers. It gleamed from the flowered plates. It filled the room. Sparks from it flew everywhere. But no! They weren't sparks. They were bees!

The small bees darted around the room, each one a golden particle of fire. The room was full of them. Miss Emmanuel had filled a copper bowl with nasturtiums, and stuffed dog-roses into pewter tankards on the dresser. But, over the brown jug on the mantlepiece, which she had filled with honey-suckle, they lingered lazily.

As Simon watched, one fell from a ripe, creamy honeysuckle trumpet and landed, heavily, on his hand. It sat there, gorged, too stupified to move. He looked down at it, and then, slowly, raised his hand

and lifted the small insect until it was close enough for him to see it properly. Its wings were beautiful. A fine, golden filigree of veins supported a delicate film which gleamed, sometimes with a hint of gold, sometimes with the promise of a rainbow.

'Humph! While we all have a good look at each other, we'd better have a little talk.' Miss Emmanuel's voice startled Simon. For one moment he had actually forgotten her. She handed him tea in a thick, willow-patterned cup and saucer, and held out a plate with two biscuits on it. 'One each!' she snapped. 'Can't spare no more.'

Simon took his biscuit and said 'thank you'.

Miss Emmanuel sat down opposite him with her tea and biscuit, and looked at him thoughtfully. 'I have to admit, Corn Du, that it was someone older than you that I expected,' she said.

'Yes, I suppose you did. I'm sorry,' Simon said. Next moment he was spilling his tea, startled by her sudden fury.

'Sorry!' she screeched. 'Sorry! Sorry for what? For being young? Don't you never say you're sorry for something you can't help. Never again. Nobody should do that. Never! Nobody! Least of all *you* . . . You're Y Corn Du, you are, and don't you forget it, *bach*.'

Simon's hands shook as he tried to sip his tea. He was making waves in his cup. Tea splashed all over

his lips. What was she calling him? . . . Y Corn Du
. . . The Black Horn . . . He didn't want to be called
that. He felt as though Miss Emmanuel was trying to
change him into a different person.

He glanced across the hearth at her. The fire lit her
face. It glistened as though it were covered with a
thin film of honey. He tried to see her eyes, but he
couldn't. She seemed to have screwed them up into
little, round holes in her head, holes which glinted
just occasionally with a quick spark of bright light.
'She's weird!' he thought. He felt very frightened.
'Why did she make them bring me here? She hasn't
said anything about helping me. All she's doing is tell
me off and stare at me.' He was glad when she began
to talk again, even though she sounded more bad-
tempered than ever.

'You never got my meaning when I was speaking to
you just now,' she said. 'Interrupted me, you did,
before I'd had my say.'

Simon nearly apologized again, but stopped himself just in time. 'I'd like to hear what else you had to
say, please,' he said instead.

'Humph,' she grunted. 'Polite aren't you, Corn
Du. Not used to such manners, I'm not. Humph!
What was I saying? Yes? You're not what I expected
because *they*—' She waved her hand at the
bees'—they said that you had power. They said as
how they could *feel* the power in you, but now that

38

I've got you here and I can see you I can *see* that it's ignorant-looking you are, not powerful-looking at all.'

'You're right,' Simon said. 'I'm sure they're wrong about me.'

She seemed to explode with fury again. 'Wrong! Wrong! My bees is never wrong!'

'B-but,' Simon began to stutter again. 'I am ignorant. I don't know how to deal with Cafall. I can't do anything about him.'

'Don't talk stupid! Of course you can deal with him. My bees is right. Power you have got, somewhere in you, and if you use what little brains you've got too, less ignorant you will be. Think, Corn Du. Think! How do you *think* you'll deal with him?'

Simon tried to think. 'I'll use my hands,' he said, 'and the black horn, I suppose.'

'Suppose! Suppose! Only suppose?' she said.

'But I *can* only suppose. I've never done anything like this before. All I *know* is that I'm going to need all the help that you are good enough to give me.'

'Good enough to give me!' she mimicked him. 'Don't you expect goodness from me, *bach*. I'm not good, never have been and never will be.' She leant forward abruptly. 'Let's see those hands,' she said.

Simon spread out his hands before her, and it seemed to him that not only Miss Emmanuel but every bee in the room came to look at them. Their

39

humming changed as they looked. They sounded interested, and then full of wonder, and, perhaps, just a little disturbed.

Miss Emmanuel tried to keep her feelings hidden. 'Humph! Yes . . . It's a useful pair of hands they are. Need a bit of strengthening and a bit of shaping up, but, yes, they're useful,' she said. She spoke casually, but Simon was almost sure that she was more impressed with his hands than she was pretending to be. He wondered what she could see in them, and wished that she would tell him, but she didn't. She just sat watching him again, with those awful little glinting eyes.

She still hasn't said anything about helping, he thought. I'm going to have to ask her if she will. 'I know that you say I'm the one who has to deal with Cafall, Miss Emmanuel,' he said, politely, 'but you will help me, won't you . . . I've got so much I need to ask you.'

'What do you want to know?' she asked suspiciously, and, suddenly, the bees were quiet.

'I want to know where Cafall came from, and what I have to do to get him to go back,' Simon said.

Miss Emmanuel stared at him speechlessly, then she shrieked with laughter. She shrieked and she cackled and the bees began to whirl around and around in a kind of frenzy.

Simon was terrified. He sat with his fists clenched

on his knees, staring at the floor. It was made of grey slate. It was the only normal thing in the room. A grey, slate floor, grey like the stones in the carn.

When Miss Emmanuel spoke to him again she sounded shocked and disgusted with him. 'Corn Du!' she said. 'It's ashamed of yourself you should be. It's pig ignorant that you are. Pig ignorant!' She looked at him craftily. 'If this was the old days, I'd have snuffed you out by now. Nipped you in the bud before you had a chance to blossom, I would have. But that sort of thing's not done no more. No! Snuffing out's no longer in the cards.' She sounded disappointed. 'I did think I might scare you silly, when I seen you standing there in all your ignorance. Yes! Scare him silly, Blod, I said, and keep him working for you for the rest of his life. But that was before I seen your hands.' She stared into her fire. 'Yes, that was before I seen your hands. But now I have seen them.' Her eyes glinted as she turned around and looked at him again. 'What I seen in your hands, Corn Du, told me that, one day, you will be much better to have for a friend than for an enemy. So I will tell you what you want to know. I will tell you what to do. But don't you forget that it was Blodwen Emmanuel that helped you in your ignorance. Don't you forget!'

Simon watched her as she leaned forward and picked up a half-burnt stick that had fallen from the

41

flames, and poked the fire with it until it blazed with a new fury. Then, suddenly, she leaned towards him and whispered frantically, as though she was almost afraid to say the words aloud. 'Cafall came from Annwn,' she told him, 'from Annwn . . .'

'Annwn?' Simon repeated the name aloud.

'Ssh!' Miss Emmanuel glanced fearfully at the window. 'Don't say you've never heard of Annwn!' She sounded horrified. Simon could only shake his head. She whispered again. 'Annwn is that place, that twilight place, where those who finished with this world long ago may be found.'

'You mean they died?'

'Ssh! Finished with *this* life,' she said. 'Use your brains! Think of Cafall. Think of how he looks. Finished with *this* world, I said.'

'It's an Underworld, is it?' Simon asked.

'Yes . . . and no.' Miss Emmanuel stared into her fire again, and Simon had to lean close to hear the words she muttered. He felt the flames hot against his face, and heard their hiss and crackle mingle with the low murmur of the bees. 'Annwn is everywhere,' she said softly. 'It is in the hills and in the valleys, beneath the earth below our feet and in the clouds above us. It is beside us and with us . . . and yet it is not *here*.'

It was very difficult. 'Then how did Cafall get *here*?

And how do I get him back into Annwn?' Simon asked.

Miss Emmanuel caught hold of his arm. Her hand gripped like a claw. She pulled him towards her until her lips were close to his ear. He could feel her breath like the movement of bees wings. She smelt of honey. 'There are certain places,' she whispered to him. 'There are certain places in this part of the world, *our* part of this world, yours *and* mine, Corn Du, there are certain places where it is possible to enter Annwn and to come out again.'

'Where are they? What do they look like?'

'A rock, a stone, a stretch of water, a tree, a wall, the back of the darkest cave—find it, move it, and there you have . . . Annwn.'

Suddenly she let go of him. Simon jerked back, his face burnt from the fire. He felt frightened, but he had to know more. 'I suppose,' he said hesitatingly, 'that the wishing well where Bethan read the spell out loud was one of those special places.'

'Suppose what you like,' Miss Emmanuel hissed at him. 'I have always made it my business not to suppose *nothing* about ways into Annwn. Best left alone, such places is. Life's safer that way.'

'But someone's got to find out about them,' Simon said.

'*You* have got to find about them. You have got to find a handy one—the same one, maybe—and put

43

that hound back through,' Miss Emmanuel told him. Her voice changed into a whine. 'It's too old I am for this caper, Corn Du. Older than your grandmother by a twelve-month, I am. If she had lived, that is. Too old to do this, I am. *You* do it, Corn Du.'

'All right.' Simon was embarrassed. She seemed to be begging. He didn't like it. 'All right,' he said, 'I'll do it. But tell me *how*. How do I open the way when I find it? And how do I get Cafall to go through?'

She sounded exasperated again then. 'How do you get a dog to go anywhere?' she said. 'Beat him! Beat him and chase him! And how do you open the way? With that spell, of course. That silly girl's got it hidden nice and safe under her bed. My bees spied it there. Get it from her, and get on with it quick—and quiet. Keep all this to yourself. Don't tell a soul, just them two and Miss Frederika, seeing she's in on it already. But no one else. Keep it to yourself.'

'All right,' Simon said, and began to stand up, but she reached forward and held on to his arm again.

'And I'll give you some advice, Corn Du,' she said. 'I'll be quite frank with you. It's too *nice* you are, too nice, too honest-looking. We can't afford to be honest and nice in this game. It's nasty you must be. Indeed yes. Nasty along with the rest of us. Rules of the game that is, especially if it's the top of the heap we're meant for, like you. Be nasty—or be snuffed out.'

Simon could only sit and stare at her. He didn't want to be nasty. He didn't want to be like that. Not like *her*. He felt shocked.

Miss Emmanuel saw that he was shocked. She began to laugh at him again. 'Never mind, *nice*, young Corn Du,' she smirked. 'Someone had to tell you the way we people have to be or you'll never survive to enjoy the power what you have stored away waiting for you in those hands.' She cackled with laughter and rocked back in her chair. '*Nice*, young Corn Du. Nice, *young* Corn Du.'

Simon wouldn't listen. He stood up and tried to walk across the room, but the bees wouldn't let him. He had to stand there, waiting for her to finish her fit of laughter and unbolt the door for him. 'Thank you,' he said coldly as he stepped up out of the room.

'Thank you, thank you!' she mimicked him again as he walked through the garden. '*Nice* young Corn Du,' she called after him, and he heard her laughter mingling with the humming of the gleaming wisp of bees that followed him as he walked into the shadow of the wood.

6
Dr Gimlett Helps Herself

Simon stumbled through the gloom of the valley feeling that he was in the middle of a nightmare which would have no end. He remembered how happy he had been as he walked home along the lane, only an hour or so ago, when he had thought that being a wizard was something that was going to happen to him far off in the future, and that magic was wonderful. It all seemed like something he had dreamed when he was very young. Now, here he was, a wizard already—and making magic was going to be dreadful.

'But surely I don't have to be like *her*,' he thought. 'Surely some people who make magic are nice. Surely some magic must be made just because it's wonderful to do. Surely it's not just done to win, to beat the others—or be beaten and snuffed out— surely there's a different way to be a wizard.' He looked neither to left nor right, wrapped in misery and worry, trying hard to think his way out of the nightmare. 'I suppose Miss Emmanuel did help quite a lot,' he thought, 'though I feel as though she's made everything twice as bad as it was before, and twice as difficult as I thought it would be. No, that's not true. She has made it easier. At least I know about Annwn now, and I know that I've got to use the spell to send

Cafall back there. I suppose I might as well get the spell from Bethan now, before I go home.'

As he opened the gate to the site-office garden, a patch of shadow broke away from the general darkness beside the porch and moved away into the dusk. Briefly, Simon saw two eyes, red in the half light, then Cafall was gone.

Simon ran the last few steps and almost leapt inside the house when Gareth opened the door.

'I know what you seen,' Gareth said. 'Awful, i'n't he!'

'Who's awful *now*?' a voice said, and Mrs Rhys came into the small hall. 'Oh hello!' she said when she saw Simon. 'I've seen you before, haven't I. Now, let me think. I know! Your dad's the new sailing instructor at the dinghy park, isn't he? And your mam's the one who made that gorgeous garden for Mrs Evans over the far side of the mountain.'

'That's right,' Simon said.

'And you are?'

'Simon,' he said. 'Simon Jones,' and felt guilty for a moment that he hadn't said Corn Du.

'Come in, Simon,' Mrs Rhys said, and pulled him into the room next to the hall.

An untidy, grey-haired woman was sitting at a table covered with a sparkling white cloth, helping herself to a huge slice of hot, meat pie. Simon remembered how Bethan had complained about a Dr Gimlett who had to be fed each evening. This must be Dr Gimlett.

She peered at him over a forkful of pie, switched on an instant, tight-lipped smile, switched it off again just as instantly, and pushed the forkful into her mouth.

Bethan had obviously been sitting opposite the blank television screen, scowling at Dr Gimlett as she waited for her to finish her meal and go. She smiled when she saw Simon, 'How did you get on?' she asked.

'All right,' Simon said.

Bethan looked at her mother warily. Mrs Rhys was listening as she lent across the table filling Dr Gimlett's glass with wine. 'Um . . . Was she all right with you?' Bethan asked, choosing her words carefully.

Simon wondered why she was being so cautious. 'Yes,' he said. 'She told me to come and ask you for the poem.'

Mrs Rhys put down the wine bottle with a thump. 'Simon! They haven't got you going with this nonsense too, have they?' she demanded.

Bethan seemed to shrink down into her chair. Gareth slipped silently out of the room. And next moment Simon understood the need for caution. Mrs Rhys stood in the middle of the room with her hands on her hips and her lips pressed tightly together. She took a deep breath, and then she told him exactly what she thought of children who believed in all the mumbo-jumbo an ignorant, uneducated, bad-tempered, old woman cared to tell them.

'It was bad enough having that pesky, stray dog hanging around off and on,' she said, 'but when you let her fill you with stories of King Arthur and magic spells . . .'

'King Arthur? Spells?' Dr Gimlett had stopped eating.

Mrs Rhys turned to face her. 'Yes,' she said apologetically, 'I'm sorry about this, Dr Gimlett, but it makes—'

'No need to apologize.' Dr Gimlett waved her glass airily, slurping wine on to the tablecloth. 'This interests me. The Arthurian legend is something of a hobby with me. And . . . er . . . well . . . *spells* are so fascinating, are they not!'

'Oh but this isn't a spell.' Mrs Rhys tried to make it all sound unimportant. 'It's nothing but a stupid sort of poem on a dirty old piece of paper.'

'Ah . . . but *is* it?' Dr Gimlett said mysteriously. She switched on her smile as she swung around in her chair to face Bethan. 'And may *I* see this spell?' she asked.

Bethan didn't want to show it to her, but she had to. Her mother told her to fetch it. 'Let Dr Gimlett see for herself what mumbo jumbo it is,' she said, so Bethan fetched it from her room.

Simon watched Dr Gimlett as she took it and unrolled it. He hadn't expected anything like this to happen. She looked so excited. She believed in magic. That was obvious. But would she believe that this was a spell? He began to worry again. What would she do if she did decide that it was a spell?

She read it quickly, her eyes flicking from side to side, her lips moving soundlessly. Even before she looked up he could see that she thought it was marvellous. She stared at Bethan, her eyes widened with excitement. 'And what did your mother say had happened, my dear?' she asked. 'A dog? There was something about a dog. Not—not Cafall? Did Cafall come when you read this?'

Bethan looked at Simon, pleading for help. He had to say something.

'Well, we're not . . . well . . . Miss Emmanuel . . .'

'Miss Emmanuel!' Mrs Rhys interrupted him. She laughed scornfully. 'Miss Emmanuel,' she told Dr Gimlett, 'is an ignorant old woman who fills their heads with fairy tales. Wishing wells, spells, Arthur's dog! Whatever next, I ask you!'

'Arthur!' Dr Gimlett said earnestly. 'Arthur next! If this child can get Cafall, *I* can get Arthur!' she said rapturously. And before anyone could say anything to stop her, she swept from the room in a flurry of long skirt and cardigan, with the spell clutched tightly in her hand.

7
Miss Emmanuel is Frightened

Just when he had found out what to do, this had happened, and now he couldn't do it. Simon stood there feeling helpless again.

Mrs Rhys was rather amazed by what had happened. She dabbed at the spilt wine with a square of kitchen towel. 'Well!' she said. 'All I can say is, it takes all sorts to make a world. And her a lady doctor too! Fancy an educated lady getting all worked up about a load of rubbish!'

Bethan pointed silently towards the door, and Simon said goodbye to Mrs Rhys and went out into the hall. There, Bethan put her finger to her lips and still wouldn't let him speak. 'Mam listens so,' she said, when they were right out in the lane, 'and she's been getting into a right old flap this last day or two, since Gareth let it slip that we'd been around to Old Blodwen's. I don't know what she'd say if she knew we'd mitched school today. You'll have to mitch, too, tomorrow, I suppose, won't you.'

Simon hadn't thought of that. He began to feel wretched about it. He had never played truant in his life. But he couldn't worry about that. He had to think about getting back the spell. He told Bethan about it. 'We'll have to get it back,' he said. 'I can't get into Annwn without it.'

'Annwn!' Bethan's voice was full of awe and wonder. 'Is that where you've got to put Cafall? Is that where he came from?'

'Yes.' Quickly, Simon told her what Miss Emmanuel had told him about the ways to Annwn.

Bethan looked around at the shadows in the lane. 'I wonder where the other places are,' she said nervously. 'And where's that Cafall lurking now? You've got to get rid of him nice and quick, Simon, please. He petrifies me, he does.'

'Well, as soon as we can think of some way to get back the spell I will,' Simon said.

He left Bethan, and began to hurry home along the lane. Suddenly, a bee came, and another, and another, and, next moment, the lane was blocked by the tall, golden column he had seen before. He couldn't go home. Miss Emmanuel wanted him to go the other way. Miss Emmanuel must want to see him again. 'Already!' Simon thought. 'She must know what's happened. She must still be spying on me.'

He did wonder, as he trudged along the lane towards the valley, if she had changed her mind about helping him, or if, maybe, she knew some way of getting back the spell. 'She might offer to ask Dr

Gimlett for it,' he thought, but had to admit to himself that this wasn't very likely. Cafall stood in the lane, but disappeared when he saw the bees. Then back into the valley Simon went, back into the gloom and darkness and the roar of rushing water.

Miss Emmanuel was waiting at her gate with a cloud of bees around her head. She didn't invite Simon to step inside. This time she raved at him there in the shadows. 'You fool, Corn Du,' she scolded as soon as she saw him. 'You fool! Letting that stupid clever-woman get away with the spell. That stupid, meddling clever-woman. Seen her sort before, I have. Seen her sort before.'

'I couldn't stop her,' Simon began to explain, then stopped. Miss Emmanuel already knew exactly what had happened.

'Got to get it back quick, you have,' she said. 'Quick! Before she gets a chance to use it.' She began to moan, and to wring her hands, twisting her skirt between her fingers. 'You don't know the trouble she could make if she gets around to meddling with the ways into Annwn. The trouble, the trouble . . . and if she don't do it right—oh-hh,' she moaned.

Simon began to feel very frightened. 'What trouble?' he asked her. 'What could she do?'

Miss Emmanuel leant over the gate whispering. 'That meddling fool,' she hissed at him. 'Don't know what she's on about, she don't. Get Arthur, she says she will. Get Arthur! As though he would be like a present for her birthday. Arthur would be worse than Cafall, Corn Du. Arthur wasn't no mincing, lily-livered, soft-voiced gentleman. Arthur was a fighting man, rough and tough and nasty as they come. If she gets that spell *right* and she gets Arthur, she'll get more than she's bargained for—and so will you, for you will never deal with Arthur, *nice* young Corn Du. Never! Arthur of the Britons would be trouble.'

'And if she gets the spell wrong?' Simon asked quietly.

'If she gets it wrong, then you and me are gone, snuffed out, Corn Du. If she get's it wrong then it is disaster.'

8

Simon Goes to Fetch the Horn

Late that evening, as Simon worked his way through his algebra homework, he wished that he could simply forget about the whole business of Cafall and Annwn and Dr Gimlett meddling with the spell. He didn't know how to be a wizard and he didn't want to know. It wasn't worth the trouble and the risk.

He went to bed and lay looking through his window at the dark shadow of the carn silhouetted against a distant galaxy, and then the moon rose, and what had been grey turned to silver, and he thought of the things he could see with Second Sight, and the wonders he had worked already with the magic of his hands, and he knew that he did want to be a wizard. He knew that it was much more important for him to try to learn to be very good at magic, than be content to be simply very good at maths.

In the morning, he felt wretched again when he pretended to get ready for school. He wished that he could just tell his father what he was really going to do, but Miss Emmanuel had said he must keep it all to himself.

One of the golden bees dashed past as he hid his school bag in the ditch beside the red dead nettles, and another stopped to look at him as he avoided the school bus stop and took the path to the caravan site instead. 'I suppose I'll have to put up with bees spying on me for ever,' he thought.

He had worked out a rough plan of what he would have to do. First of all, he would fetch the black horn. Miss Emmanuel had said nothing about using it, but he wanted it. Fred was always telling him that it was his. Well, all right, he hadn't agreed with her before, but now he did. He wanted it, and he would get it before he did anything else. 'Miss Emmanuel's calling me Corn Du, so I'll carry it to show every-body that that's who I am,' he thought. 'But who will there be to show? Fred, Bethan, Gareth, Dr Gimlett —Arthur?' He hoped not Arthur.

He began to think about Fred. He had to tell her everything that had happened after she left him. He had a feeling Fred would be a great help when he tried to get back the spell. 'As long as she doesn't try to rush me,' he thought. 'She mustn't rush me.'

He wished that he had thought of arranging to meet Bethan and Gareth somewhere. He had to keep Bethan with him, because he would need to keep Cafall near him. 'But not too near,' he thought. 'I'll keep him at a safe distance until the last moment, when the way to Annwn is open and I'm ready to deal with him.' He couldn't think of any way in which he could possibly deal with Cafall without help, but decided not to worry about that until he had to.

He hurried along beside the caravan site, looking for Bethan and Gareth. But it was Dr Gimlett whom he saw. She came, almost skipping, out of her caravan with the spell in her hand. 'She mustn't see me!' Simon looked around, desperately, for somewhere to hide.

'Simon! Ssh. Over here. Quick!' Bethan waved frantically from behind a patch of brambles and Simon scrambled through them quickly. Gareth was there too, and so was Cafall. Bethan and Gareth seemed to feel exactly as Simon did about Cafall.

They were trying very hard not to touch him. Bethan noticed that Simon was keeping well away from him. 'He won't hurt you,' she whispered. 'He's getting tame—I think. But he's not real, sort of, is he? That's what makes it so scary.'

They waited until Dr Gimlett had gone on along the lane, then hid Bethan's school bag, and began to follow her. They couldn't persuade Gareth to hide his satchel. 'Me dinner's in it,' he said, and refused to let go of it.

'Dr Gimlett's sure to be at the wishing well,' Simon said, as soon as Bethan had given up trying to pull the satchel out of Gareth's hands. 'We'll have to pass her.'

'She's no worry,' Bethan said. 'We can sneak behind the bushes and dodge her. It's Mam who's the worry. She mustn't see us mitching, and, most of all, she mustn't see Cafall again.'

'She's going to tell the p'lice if she sees him hanging around today,' Gareth said. 'So's Tad. And Tad's going to tell the farmers to watch out for him too.'

'It's all getting worse,' Simon thought. 'We'll have to keep hidden,' he said to Bethan.

They didn't go near Miss Emmanuel's cottage, but, as they passed the end of the valley, two bees came darting close to Simon, and a small swarm of them flushed out Cafall from among the ferns where he had been creeping along behind them. Cafall didn't like the bees. He ran off into the wood and was still far away when they reached the wishing well. Dr Gimlett was too busy with the spell to notice any rustling of bushes. They crept along, out of sight, stopping for a moment, to try to listen to what she was saying, but she was too far away to be heard.

Simon listened to her droning voice, and began to worry. Perhaps he should try to get back the spell before he fetched the horn. Perhaps that was the most important thing to do first. 'I wonder if we could get closer,' he whispered to Bethan, peering between the branches of a laurel bush. 'What's she doing? I can't see her very well.'

Bethan pushed him aside and parted the branches a little. 'Cripes! She's on her knees!' she said. 'Whatever's she doing? Oh, I see! She'd dropped the spell. Lucky she missed the mud! Ah, that's it! I can see what's the matter now. She's having trouble with holding it open. You'd have thought she'd be able to manage that. I've never seen anybody so clumsy as she is. Real cack-handed! What's she doing now? Oo, Simon, she's coming over by here. Ssh! Keep quiet!'

They crouched in the bushes, as Dr Gimlett picked her way to a large rock, sat down on it, spread the spell on her knees, and began to practise it.

'*By Saturn,*
By Uranus . . .' she began . . .

'No! That's not right! There's an i in there ... *By Uran-i-us* ... Drat!'

'The paper's rolled up again,' Bethan whispered.

'She's not going to get very far with it like that, is she?'

'No,' Simon said. 'All the same, I wonder if we ought to try to get it back?'

'Pinch it back, do you mean?' Bethan said.

'Oh we couldn't do that.'

'Why not? She pinched it from us.'

'Do you think we could? But how?'

'Just nip out and grab it.'

'Could we?'

'I'm game to try. Come on! No wait! Somebody's coming.'

Simon crouched back in the bushes with Gareth while Bethan stood quite still and watched.

'Who is it?' Simon whispered.

'It's a man. I think it's Fred's tad. Yes, it is, Oo! Dr Gimlett's all embarrassed. She's rolling up the spell. She's all of a fluster. She's getting up as though she wasn't doing anything special. Aw, she's going back down the lane with him. We won't be able to get it now.'

For a moment, Simon wondered if he could step out and tell Guy about the spell and ask him to get it back from Dr Gimlett. But he remembered that Miss Emmanuel had told him not to tell anyone else about it all, and it didn't seem a very good idea anyway. 'Oh well, that's that,' he said. 'At least she's stopped trying for a while. But I think we'd better hurry.'

They scrambled back on to the path, and ran until they reached the stile where the lane joined the road. A sports car was parked there, with its wheels on the grass verge.

'That's Guy's Morgan,' Simon said. 'I wonder why he was walking down the lane?'

Fred said exactly the same thing when they met her. 'What's Guy doing in that lane, I wonder? He's supposed to be driving to the village for a paper.' She shrugged her shoulders. 'He felt in need of a walk, poor old thing, I suppose,' she said. She looked at Simon brightly. 'Well?' she asked. 'How are you getting on with it?'

'Not too well,' Simon said, and told her what had happened.

Fred was furious about Dr Gimlett. 'Of all the interfering old busy-bodies!' she said. 'I hate people who poke their noses into somebody else's business. And to run off with the spell without so much as asking!'

'Arthur's her hobby,' Simon said. 'She's very keen, you see. She even knew Cafall's name, which is something I didn't know. And she knew about Annwn.'

'I wonder how much else she knows,' Fred said. 'I wonder if she knows about there being other ways into Annwn as well as the one she's trying.'

'She can't know that,' Simon began to worry again.

'Why not? I know about them. Meryl read me stories about them years ago. I don't know where they are, of course, but I'm sure I could make a few good guesses.' Fred frowned. 'What I'm getting at, Jonesy, is that if she doesn't get good results at the wishing well she might go off to try somewhere else, and then you won't know where she is, and you'll have lost the spell altogether.'

'Somebody's going to have to stay and keep an eye on her,' Bethan said.

'Who?' Fred asked.

Fred and Bethan decided that the only one who could be spared was Gareth. He didn't want to leave them, but Bethan told him that he must. 'We won't be long,' she said. 'All you have to do is keep an eye on Dr Gimlett, see, without letting her see you. And when we come back we'll coo-ee until we find you.'

He looked very small as he ran off, back along the lane, all on his own, clutching his dinner satchel tightly under his arm. Simon began to worry about him. 'I can't really see the need for him to go,' he said. 'Are you sure he'll be all right?'

'Aw, don't worry about Gareth,' Bethan said confidently. 'He's tough, he is, even if he's small. He knows his way around all the lanes too, *and* he's clever.'

'Yes, but he doesn't really need to go . . .' Simon

began. He knew that Miss Emmanuel would soon send her bees to fetch him if he lost Dr Gimlett and couldn't find her on his own, but he didn't really want to have to go to see her again if he could possibly manage not to, so he didn't argue.

'Of course we need him to go,' Fred said. 'Bethan can't. She's got to stay with you to keep Cafall here. And I've got to get the horn for you.'

Simon didn't think this made sense, but Fred obviously had it all planned. He did wonder if he was letting her rush him but, when they reached the avenue to Tŷ Corn Du, he stopped worrying altogether. He forgot about Gareth. He forgot about Dr Gimlett. He forgot about Miss Emmanuel. He even forgot about Fred and Bethan and Cafall who were there with him. Suddenly he was alone. He was alone in this beautiful avenue which led to the place which had been the home of the First Wizard of the Black Horn.

He looked at the pale, slender trunks of the tall beech trees, and then gazed up at the blur of green and bronze and blue where the late summer leaves seemed to mingle with the sky. This was a magic place, and as much like home to him as was the mountain.

'I'll go to the summer house,' he thought.

Vaguely, he heard Fred call to him. 'I'll fetch the

horn.' He noticed her say something to Bethan and saw them both begin to run.

He looked up for a moment at the beautiful old house, then made his way around it, treading softly on the thyme-filled lawn. The garden glowed with the rich colours of chrysanthemums and the gold of late daisies. He passed the sundial, pushed his way through the overgrown lavender, and scrambled into the summer house.

It was there that Fred handed him the black horn. 'This is where you first used it, Jonesy,' she said. She was very excited. Simon saw Bethan, wide-eyed, peering over her shoulder. Cafall was there too, standing, silently, watching him.

'I know it is,' Simon said. 'This was the very first place.'

Then he took the black horn from Fred, and turned to face the mountain. With the horn in his hands he could *see* the mountain. He didn't have to imagine it. He could see every single stone of the carn, every path, every patch of bilberry and heather. He looked at it now, and as he looked he felt the power that was in his hands bring the horn to life. And he knew as he felt it, that Fred had been right when she argued about the horn. Of course he should keep it near him. It was almost as though it was part of him. It was *his*. How could he ever have doubted it?

9

Gareth Disappears and Miriam Tries to Help

Fred decided that Bedwyr must be shut in while Cafall was there. 'And I'm not going to ride Gwenhwyfar again either, until you've got him back into Annwn,' she told Simon, 'just to be on the safe side. And now let's hurry and catch up with Gareth and Dr Gimlett, and see if we can't do something, between us, to get back the spell. Let's hurry. Let's get it over.' She caught hold of Bethan's hand, and, together, they ran back along the avenue.

Simon ran behind them, glad to be hurrying. He had an idea that he had somehow infected them with his feeling of awe and wonder at the magic of Tŷ Corn Du and the black horn in his hands. They were quiet. Somehow they were sobered by the sudden importance of it all.

And when they reached the wishing well, suddenly, it all became not only important but much more serious—and more frightening than ever.

Dr Gimlett wasn't there. Nor was Gareth. But his satchel lay on a patch of wet earth right in front of the well. And the ground all around it was strewn with apple blossom.

Bethan picked up the satchel and began to call frantically. 'Coo-ee. Coo-ee.' But Fred filled her hands with blossom and turned to face Simon. She didn't speak. She simply held it out to him. Her face was whiter than the blossom in her hands. Her eyes were open wide with wonder.

'I can't make him hear.' Bethan's lips were quivering as though she was going to cry. Then she noticed the blossom. 'Apple blossom?' she cried. 'But it's autumn nearly, and there aren't any apple trees by here . . .' She stopped. She had remembered something. 'Avalon!' she said to Simon. 'Avalon! That was one of the words in the spell. And in school Sir says there was apple trees in Avalon.'

'Jonesy.' Fred's voice was no more than a whisper. 'Dr Gimlett made it work. She opened the way. Do—do you think she called out Arthur?'

'I don't know,' Simon said. 'I don't know.' Were Avalon and Annwn the same place? He didn't know that either. And the thought of Arthur, the Arthur that Miss Emmanuel had described to him, was terrifying. Arthur and Cafall to deal with . . . if she got the spell right. 'But did she get it right?' he wondered. And then he began to think about Gareth. He stared at the satchel hopelessly. 'It was right in front of the well,' he thought. 'Right in front of the well.' He had an awful feeling that Gareth could be lost, not in this world, but in Annwn. 'Lost for ever,' he thought, and felt even more despondent.

They stood there in the lane calling Gareth, but he didn't come. Bethan was nearly frantic with worry about him, but Simon was fairly certain that she hadn't even begun to think that he might possibly be lost in Annwn, so he didn't mention it. Fred, however, was wondering if that might be where he was. Simon knew that as soon as she said: 'Well, he *could* be somewhere else with Dr Gimlett, of course. We might as well go and look for her. It's worth a try. We're not getting anywhere just standing here shouting coo-ee.'

A small skein of bees darted away as they began to walk on. Simon watched them nervously. He was expecting the golden column to appear at any moment, to make him go to see Miss Emmanuel. 'She will know exactly what has happened,' he thought. 'The bees will have seen it all. She's sure to have some new instructions, or something, for me now.'

He looked around carefully, but there was no golden column, in fact, he couldn't even see one single bee. He couldn't understand it. Something had definitely happened back there at the wishing well. The apple blossom proved that. So why wasn't Miss Emmanuel sending for him?

He decided, when he had thought about it for a while, that it must be because whatever had happened wasn't important to Miss Emmanuel.

What ever had happened didn't make any difference to what she had already told him to do. He still had to get the spell away from Dr Gimlett and put Cafall back into Annwn. 'It must mean that Dr Gimlett is still in this world, still with the spell—and still without Arthur. Miss Emmanuel would be sure to want to warn me about Arthur. At least, I think she would. But what about Gareth? Would she want to tell me if he had gone into Annwn?' He decided that she wouldn't, for, to Miss Emmanuel, whatever happened to Gareth would be of no importance whatsoever.

As they came near the caravan site, Bethan began to worry about her mother. 'If Mam sees me out of school, I'll be for it,' she said. 'And if she finds out I've lost our Gareth she'll half kill me.'

'Perhaps you'd better wait here,' Fred said. 'And you, Jonesy. You're mitching too, aren't you, but I'm still on holiday. It's safe for me to be seen. I'll go on and have a look around.'

Cafall came slinking from behind an old stone wall while they waited for Fred to come back. He lay in a patch of shade in the middle of the lane, and watched them.

'He looks as though he's made of shadow, sometimes,' Bethan said. 'Funny, he is. He looks like a shadow, but you can feel he's there. Scary, he is. I

68

must say I'm glad he's staring at *you* most of the time, now, Simon, not just at me all the time.'

'Is he?'

'Yes! Hadn't you noticed? Ever since he seen you take the horn, back there at Fred's, he's been real interested in you.'

'He must know about the black horn!' Simon looked at Cafall with new interest. 'How can he know about the horn?' he wondered.

He hadn't time to think about it before Fred came back. She beckoned and called to them. 'Come on!

The coast's all clear. I was just in time to see Mrs Rhys drive off in a cloud of dust.'

'Was Gareth with her?' Bethan asked.

'No, she was on her own. I can't see your father anywhere, or any of the groundsmen, so you're safe enough. The only trouble is that we really need to find someone to ask about Dr Gimlett.'

'She might be in her caravan.'

'Shall I have a look?' Fred asked. 'Which one's hers? I'll ring the bell and think of some excuse if she does come out.'

Fred rang Dr Gimlett's bell several times, but no one came. All that happened, was that Poor Miriam looked out of her window and then dodged back again. Simon and Bethan both saw her.

'What about asking her?' Bethan said. 'She doesn't miss much that goes on, Mam says. She might even have noticed if Gareth came past.'

'We'll ask her,' Fred said. 'Come on!'

This time, Bethan rang the bell. Poor Miriam didn't open the door at first, so Bethan rang again, and then again, and, at last, the door opened a very little way, and a very anxious-looking face peered out. When she saw that it was Bethan standing there, Poor Miriam seemed to relax. She pulled the door open, smiling. 'It's *you*!' she said. 'My word, are you for it! Your mother's out to get your scalp,' she said. She stepped forward, and then she saw Fred, and immediately she was shy and anxious again. 'Oh! It's Fred too. I didn't see you . . .' she began.

But Bethan wanted to hear more about her mother. 'What's Mam mad for?' she said. 'What's she found out?'

'Oh-ho! There speaks a guilty conscience!' Poor Miriam laughed in spite of her nervousness. 'Have you done more than play hooky, and leave your best school bag in the brambles, and take a stray dog off somewhere so that she won't see it?'

Bethan looked as though she was going to cry. 'I've lost Gareth too,' she said.

Poor Miriam frowned. 'Oh dear! Hasn't he gone to school either?'

'I suppose you haven't seen if he went along the lane?' Fred asked. 'He might be with Dr Gimlett, we think.'

'Oh no, he's definitely not with Dr Gimlett,' Poor Miriam said, and now she looked embarrassed, but rather amused too.

'How do you know that?' Simon had been standing away from the caravan door, slightly on one side. Now he moved forward beside Fred and Bethan, and Miriam noticed him for the first time. Next moment she noticed the black horn too.

And Simon was sure, as he watched her face, that Miriam knew all about him and the horn. She stared at the horn, and then she looked at his face, carefully, like his mother did when she was trying to decide whether he was working too hard or if he wasn't well. 'Is something wrong?' she asked him. 'Is . . . is something happening?'

Simon was sure that by 'something', Miriam meant 'something magic'. But how could she know? How could she know about him? Was she like Miss Emmanuel?

Simon couldn't answer. He stared back at her. She looked nice. He liked the look of her. But how could she know about him? He had never met her. He had only seen her once before. He tried to think of something to say. He mustn't tell her anything. Miss Emmanuel had said he must keep it all secret. And if Miriam was another 'woman who knew everything' he must be even more careful to keep it secret from *her*. Desperately, he tried to think of something to say, and he felt that, all the time that he was thinking, Miriam was holding her breath in anticipation. Finally, he asked her a question. 'Why do you think that something might be happening?' he asked.

Miriam answered carefully. 'Because I'm putting two and two together, Simon. There was the most awful scene here a few minutes ago, which I couldn't help but witness. It began with Dr Gimlett coming along the lane with the most beautiful spray of apple blossom I have ever had the joy to see. She met Mrs Rhys just by the stile. I didn't realize it right away, but Mrs Rhys must just have had a phone call from the school asking why Bethan and Gareth weren't there, and had gone out to look for them and found the school bag. She said all this to Dr Gimlett. Shouted it, rather. I couldn't help but hear. Anyway . . .' Miriam began to speak very carefully now, as though she was remembering what she had heard and thinking about it in a different way, now that she had seen Simon with the black horn in his hands. 'Mrs Rhys accused Dr Gimlett of encouraging you children in a lot of nonsense. She said that it was Dr Gimlett's fault that you hadn't gone to school, and she knew what you would be doing. You would be hiding that stray wolfhound somewhere, and she was going to phone the police right away and report it. And when Dr Gimlett heard that she went beserk. She began to shout—well, to raise her voice, really I suppose . . . She started laying down the law. On no account was Mrs Rhys to report that hound. It *was* Cafall, she said.' Miriam seemed slowly to realize the significance of the name. 'Oh lor . . . Cafall!' she said, and looked exactly like Fred had as she held out the apple blossom to Simon.

'Are you all right?' Fred stepped forward quickly, and, for one moment, Simon thought that she was going to put her arm around Miriam.

Miriam smiled at her. 'Yes, I'm all right, Fred. It's just, well, a bit startling.'

73

'What happened next?' Simon wanted to make her hurry.

'Well, Dr Gimlett waved the apple blossom at Mrs Rhys and said: "Look at this. Look! It worked. I made it work. I'll get *him* yet. I'll try somewhere else . . ." '

'Try somewhere else!' Simon was appalled. 'She knows there are other places!'

'But Gareth wasn't there. Are you sure you never seen Gareth?' Bethan's voice sounded different. Simon glanced at her quickly. She looked suspicious. She didn't trust Miriam. He could see that she didn't.

Miriam didn't seem to notice. She shook her head. 'All I saw was your mother and Dr Gimlett, and your mother has now gone rushing off to see "that Jones boy's mother".' She turned to Simon. 'That means you're for it too, Simon, I suppose, though that's hardly important at the moment, is it?'

'No, it isn't,' Fred said. 'But what is important is have you any idea where Dr Gimlett has gone?'

'Yes, I have,' Miriam said. 'Dr Gimlett shouted, rather dramatically, that she was going to the top of that wonderful mountain. I suppose that means that she's gone up to the carn.'

It was a shock. If Miriam had hit him, Simon couldn't have felt more sudden fear and, almost, pain.

'Oh dear! Is that bad?' Miriam asked. She was looking at his face closely again.

Simon couldn't answer her, but Fred did. 'It's a very special place,' she said. 'No one should interfere with it.'

'Then you must stop her,' Miriam said. 'You'd better get a move on. Shall I come too?' she asked Simon.

'No!' Simon said quickly—too quickly. Miriam looked offended. 'No thank you.' He tried to be polite. He turned abruptly, and began to stalk away. Bethan turned away with him, glancing back over her shoulder at Miriam. Fred stopped to say 'good bye', and then hurried after them.

'Hurry!' Bethan said to her. 'Get away from her.'

'Why?' Fred looked amazed.

'She's a witch!' Bethan said. 'Another one! One that doesn't even belong here.'

'She never is!' Fred looked upset. 'She's nice! Anybody with half an eye in their head could see what a nice person she is.'

'Then how did she know all about you? How did she know your name? And Simon's? *And* she knew all about the black horn. You could see she did.'

'Well, well—she must know somebody we know,' Fred said. 'Yes, that's it! That must be it. What do you think, Jonesy?'

'Yes, that must be it,' Simon said. 'But let's get away from her, just in case.' He was as worried as Bethan was about Miriam, but not as scared, for Fred was right, he was almost sure she was, when she said that Miriam was nice. She was sensible too. Could she have helped? No! He couldn't ask. He must keep it all secret. She knew more than Miss Emmanuel would approve of already, he was sure. No, he must just get on with it all on his own. And he must hurry! Dr Gimlett on the carn with the spell! He could hardly dare to think about it. Dr Gimlett on the carn . . . The carn—the most magic of all magic places.

'I must stop her before she gets there. She mustn't use it there.' He gripped the horn until it began to burn his hands. 'If she uses the spell up there and gets it *right*, then she *will* get Arthur. And if she uses it up there and gets it *wrong* then, just as Miss Emmanuel said, it will be disaster . . . '

10
Dr Gimlett on the Mountain

The mountain was different. A dark plume of cloud curled angrily above the carn. Simon saw it as they crossed the estuary, and, as he looked at it, he knew that the mountain wouldn't feel like home any more.

When they reached the village, he looked up again, and it was as if he saw a hand reach out and pluck the grey cloud from the sky and wrap it, like a cloak of darkness, around the summit of the mountain. The carn was hidden. And when they reached the mountain's lower slopes the cloud had begun to slide among the hawthorn trees and fill the gateways to the fields with strange, grey shapes.

Bethan was holding tightly to Fred's hand. She looked very frightened. 'Cafall looks terrible in this,' she said. 'Look!'

They all turned around. The great hound, his head thrust forward, his eyes gleaming red in the strange, half light, came padding silently behind them. A wisp of cloud slid, snake-like, about his legs, and for a moment he seemed nothing but a great, grey head, staring at them from nowhere.

'Jonesy,' Fred sounded scared. 'I suppose all this means that Dr Gimlett beat us to the carn, doesn't it?' Simon nodded. 'Well, in that case,' Fred said, 'there's not much point in going any farther, is there. I mean, it's no use trying to stop her any more, up there, so couldn't we just wait in your garden until she comes back down? I don't fancy going any farther.'

'I've got to go on,' Simon said. 'I think she's got the spell wrong. I think I ought to find out what happened. I'll probably have to do something about it, you see, so I'll have to know about it quickly. But you go in, if you like. You could take Bethan in. I think Cafall might stay with me without her now.'

'I'm not going in anywhere,' Bethan said. 'Our Gareth might be up there in this.' She began to call him. 'Gareth, Gareth. Coo-ee . . .' It was like the cry of a lost, wild bird.

'I couldn't go in and leave you,' Fred said. She had begun to sound terrified now. 'But it's dangerous, Jonesy, up there in all this cloud.'

Simon knew that it was dangerous. But it wasn't the danger of being lost in the cloud that frightened him. He was afraid of whoever it was that owned the hand he had seen pull the cloud on to the mountain. It was as though he could *feel* that someone evil was in the cloud. He shivered. The cloud seemed to seep through him, right to the back of his mind. He felt

numb, almost frozen, but his hands were warm, and the black horn still throbbed with life. He gripped it tightly, and walked forward along the gradually steepening path.

He almost fell over Dr Gimlett. She was crouching in the middle of the track, huddled pathetically, hugging her cardigan around her body. She was shivering, and her face seemed to gleam with a terrible, translucent whiteness.

They crowded around her, but she didn't seem to see them until Fred and Bethan tried to lift her to her feet. Then she looked around, startled, as though she had just woken up. 'It's the children,' she murmured. Then she seemed to remember something, and, instantly, she looked terrified. 'I must get off the mountain,' she whispered frantically. 'I must get off the mountain . . . or I'll . . . I'll turn into something.'

'What?' Fred said. She was shivering too. 'What did you say?'

'I'll turn into something.' Dr Gimlett looked around wildly, still whispering. 'It was a spell . . . another spell . . . a spell on *me*. I couldn't understand it, but it was a spell. I'll turn into something. I *know*!' She struggled to stand up, grabbing at Fred and Bethan in a desperate effort to pull herself from the ground. Something fell from her left hand—a crumpled ball of paper.

Fred pounced on it and grabbed it. 'I've got it!' she whispered triumphantly to Simon. 'I've got our spell.'

'Yes,' Simon said, vaguely. He peered hopelessly into the cloud.

'Now you can do everything you've got to do.'

'I can't.' Simon shook his head. 'I can't . . . not now.'

'Why not?' Fred wailed at him.

'It's too late. Didn't you understand what Dr Gimlett said? She called someone out of Annwn, up on the carn. She called out someone who can cast spells . . . Well, I can't cast spells. I couldn't have pulled down this cloud from the sky. This wizard, or whoever it is, is much better at magic than I am. I can't do anything. All that will happen now is that I will be snuffed out . . .'

11

Twm Cymylau

Fred and Bethan stared at Simon, horrified. Then Bethan began to cry hysterically. 'You've *got* to do something,' she sobbed. 'You've got to. There's nobody else can, only you, Old Blod said, and the bees. Oh, and what if our Gareth's up there mixed up with it all!'

80

'Jonesy!' Fred caught hold of Simon's arm and shook him. 'You won't be snuffed out. You've got the black horn. You can fight with that. You can't just give in.'

'I can't fight,' Simon said. 'I don't know what to do. It's no use my facing up to someone as good at magic as this.'

Fred stamped her foot with exasperation. 'You must be able to do something. Think, Jonesy, think!'

It was what Miss Emmanuel had said to him. Simon bowed his head over the horn and told her what he had known from the beginning. 'I need help,' he said. 'I know I need help.'

'Right!' Fred said. '*We'll* help, Bethan and me.'

'But you can't! You haven't any magic.'

Fred wouldn't listen. 'Of course we can help! We'll be able to do *something*. Come on!'

They half carried Dr Gimlett as far as Simon's house, and pushed her through the gate, and told her to knock on the front door. Then they ran away. They heard Simon's mother come out and call. 'Simon, Simon!' But they ran on.

'Where are we going?' Bethan shouted to Fred.

'Out of this cloud,' Fred called back. 'We've got to get out of this cloud.'

She was right. Simon realized that. The cloud was overpowering. It made him feel beaten before the real fight had even begun. They ran to the end of the lane. It seemed less dense there. He slowed down. It didn't seem right, to be running away from his mountain. He ought to think. 'We'd better stop,' he called to Fred. 'We'd better stop and think about what to do next.'

Fred stopped running. 'All right,' she said, breathlessly. 'We'll stop and practise the spell.'

'Should we?'

'Of course we should!'

Cafall caught up with them and stood between Bethan and Simon as they huddled beneath an overgrown buddleia bush on the hedge by the church and smoothed out the crumpled paper.

Fred read the spell aloud. She kept her voice low, and Simon knew that she was fearful, but perhaps just a little hopeful too, that she might make it work.

'*By Saturn to me,*' Fred read,

'*By Uranius,*

By Sadak, Melik,

Skat, Aquarius.

From Annwn, Avalon or Lyonesse,

From cave across the ocean Atlantesse.

To me by moonlight,

Starlight, Light of Day

I bid thee come to me.

Come,

Come my way.'

They waited. Nothing happened.

'It never worked, and good job too,' Bethan said. 'You got it right first time, though.'

'That's something, I suppose,' Fred said. She looked at Simon. 'Now you are going to practise it,' she said.

She was rushing him. Simon wished she wouldn't do that. He wanted to think. He looked back along the lane. The cloud was thickening. Should he stop and practise the spell? Or should he run farther away first? He couldn't decide.

Fred made up his mind for him. She looked across the road at the churchyard. 'What about trying it there?' she said. 'It's a very ancient holy place. Meryl says it was even special long before the church was built on it. You never know, it might be one of the doorways.'

Simon looked across at the churchyard, too. It lay, neat and tidy, behind its high, stone wall. It didn't seem the right place for a spell, but if it was ancient and special, it might be a door into Annwn, just like Fred said. He made up his mind. 'All right. It won't hurt to have a quick practice, but it must be quick, and if it should work . . . well, Cafall might go back.'

The iron gate creaked as they pushed it open. They walked a little way along the path, then stopped. The cloud seemed to have thickened rapidly. Simon didn't like it. It slipped among the tombstones, and wisped away, up past the church tower.

'I'll hold the spell for you.' Nervously, Fred began to organize him. 'Bethan, you get Cafall to stand by Jonesy, if you can. That's it! Right, I think we're ready. Now, off you go,' she said to Simon.

It didn't feel right. This wasn't the way to make magic. He should be on his own. Fred shouldn't be rushing him. But she was trying to help, and he must practise the spell . . . At least, it seemed sense to practise it. He peered at the paper. 'I can't see it,' he said. Fred held it closer to his eyes, and he began to read. '*By Saturn to me, By Uranius . . .*' He faltered. This wasn't right! This was stupid! He should be chanting this spell, shouting it bravely. He would practise it once, then he would learn it off by heart. He read on. '*By Sadak, Melik, Skat, Aquarius . . .*'

A low, unpleasant laugh came flowing like oil through the greyness that surrounded them. They hadn't heard the gate creak, but surely the person who laughed must have come through the gate, for it seemed to be a real person that stood there among the graves. And it seemed to Simon that he and that person were the only people there. Fred and Bethan seemed to have faded away. He was alone with that dark figure, shrouded in its long, black, hooded gown.

It wasn't until he heard him speak that he realized that the person was a man, not a woman. He couldn't understand a word he said, but he knew

what he meant. He knew from the bantering, scornful tone of his voice that the man was making fun of him ... and he knew why. It was because he, the one who held in his hands the black horn with all its power, didn't even know how to say a spell.

The man seemed to find it all exciting. He spoke rapidly, shrugging his shoulders eloquently, from time to time and shaking his head vigorously in mock horror at Simon's ignorance. And, as he shook his head, the loose hood of his gown slipped back and fell in folds around his shoulders and Simon saw his face.

It was a cruel face, with thick, arched eyebrows and eyes narrowed to hide the viciousness and deceit that must show in them. It was greedy too, with flaccid cheeks and heavy jowls. And it was white as though it never saw the light of day. But, worst of all, it was young.

'Sixth form!' Simon thought. 'He would be in the sixth form. He's not much older than me . . . and he's weird already . . . and nasty.'

The young man jerked up his hood, irritably, as though he was furious at being seen. Then, quickly, he was composed again. He stood still, facing Simon, his arms folded, his hands thrust deep into his sleeves. For a few moments, he stood like that. Then, suddenly, he flung his arms wide.

He had a wand. With a movement as swift as the blink of an eyelid, he raised it, and he laughed . . . It was then that Cafall growled.

Simon had forgotten Cafall. He looked down. He saw the white fangs bared, the eyes glittering with hatred, the muscles rippling as he crouched to spring.

'He'll tear him apart! He mustn't! I can't let him . . . No!' he shouted, and swept the Black Horn in a great curve. It cut the cloud. It struck the earth at Cafall's feet. And lightning sprang singing through the air.

The young man disappeared. No one saw him go. But when the blinding flash of light had melted away, he was no longer there.

'He's vanished,' Bethan whispered. 'You beat him, Simon. You scared off Twm Cymylau.'

'Who?' Simon said. 'You knew him! You knew his name!'

Bethan nodded. 'Twm Cymylau,' she repeated. '*Everybody* knows about Twm. He *gets* you if you don't behave yourself. *Everybody* knows that.'

Simon looked at Fred. 'Do *you* know about him?' he asked.

'Yes,' Fred said. 'He's the local bogyman. You know! All the grannies say: "If you don't do as I tell you Twm Cymylau will get you." Meryl told me about him. He was *horrible*. He was a boy who was found on the mountain one winter, half dead from exposure. No one knew where he came from, or where he went in the end, either, but while he was here he was absolutely *evil*. He made terrible magic and terrified everybody for miles around, and kept the whole place wrapped in mist for seven years, too. Cattle got lost in it, boats were wrecked, fruit wouldn't ripen. In fact, everything awful that could happen because of mist did happen.'

'And lots of children got lost for ever,' Bethan said, 'an' anybody grown up that he met in the mist he did in.'

'Snuffed them out,' Simon said, 'just like he'll snuff out me.' He looked at Fred again. She looked back at him but said nothing. Fred knew, as well as Simon did, that it was sheer luck that he had managed to trick Twm Cymylau. He hadn't beaten him. He hadn't really frightened him away. Twm would be back. And next time he would try a little harder to make the evil magic that he so obviously intended to make.

12
Flight from the Cloud

'You do need help, don't you,' Fred said.

Simon nodded. 'But there isn't anyone to ask,' he said. 'I've got to think of something to do on my own.'

'When he comes back you'll have to be nastier,' Fred said.

Bethan had been listening to them. Now she sounded terrified. 'You mean you never beat Twm?' she said.

'Of course he didn't beat him!' Fred was so frightened she began to feel angry. 'He could have. He could have let Cafall get him. Cafall would have kept us safe.' She turned on Simon. 'You should have let him. You should have. If he comes back you must.'

Simon could only shake his head in despair.

'Well, what are you going to do, then? Think! For goodness sake think.'

'Let's run again,' Simon said. 'Let's get away from the cloud again.'

'Let's run to Miss Emmanuel,' Fred said.

'That wouldn't do any good,' Simon said. 'She's given me all the help she wants to.'

'How do you know? She might have changed her mind.'

'If she wanted me for anything she would send a column of bees.'

Fred stamped her foot. 'You're afraid of her! That's what's the matter isn't it. You're afraid of her.'

'No!' Simon protested. 'No! I'm not afraid of her . . . not much. I just know she won't help.'

Bethan began to cry. 'You said we ought to run. Let's go. Please, let's just run and find somewhere safe.'

'Miss Emmanuel's!' Fred said. 'There's no one else to run to.'

Simon gave in. 'All right,' he said. 'We'll run to Miss Emmanuel.' There was nothing else he could do. 'While we're running Fred won't rush me,' he thought. 'I'll have time to think.'

They kept close together as they made their way out of the churchyard. Even Cafall stayed close. He had never been so close. There was a change in Cafall. Before, he had slunk after them, but now he ran with them.

Bethan soon noticed the change. 'Simon!' she said. 'Cafall's with you. Look at him!'

Fred sounded almost excited. 'He's different!' she said. 'There's no lurk about him now. He's just like he must be with Arthur. It's because you used the horn like that, Jonesy. It must be.'

Simon hardly noticed what they were saying. He was concentrating on this urgent need for help. If only he could find someone. But who? There was no one. He was going to have to manage, somehow.

He had a vague idea that the best thing he could do would be to get up to the carn, and wait there, ready to chant the spell and open the door into Annwn as soon as the terrible Twm Cymylau came back, and then, somehow, trick or persuade him to go through. 'Perhaps I could let Cafall loose on him,' he thought, but he didn't like that idea.

He hurried through the village with Fred and Bethan. It was like a drowned city. The headlights of cars on the main road gleamed dimly, like the eyes of monsters swimming sluggishly through deep, grey water. People, like shadow figures, took shape for a moment, then melted away again. They recognized no one. Once, Bethan thought she saw Miriam in her car, and Simon felt anxious for a moment, but no one else saw her, and he soon forgot her again.

There was no cloud on the estuary. They ran across the sand beneath a clear, blue sky.

'Could we just go to our place and see if Gareth's there, do you think?' Bethan asked.

'All right. But we mustn't let Miriam see us,' Simon said.

'But she might have noticed him,' Fred argued. 'We could just slip in and leave you in the lane.'

'I'm not going near her,' Bethan said flatly. 'I just want to slip in to our place.'

'You're stupid about Miriam!' Fred was beginning to sound angry again. 'She could help. *I* think she would.'

They didn't go near Miriam or the site office. They couldn't. As they ran into the lane, a wisp of cloud reached out from the ditch beneath the hedge and twined around Simon's ankles.

Fred wailed. 'He's coming after us!'

'All right!' Simon could see that she was going to panic. He didn't know what to say to her. 'All right!' He tried to sound calm. 'We'll just have to keep ahead of him. Come on! We'll soon be at Miss Emmanuel's.' He didn't really think that Miss Emmanuel would help, but he did think that she might let them shelter with her. She would know how to keep herself safe from someone like Twm Cymylau. She would be able to keep them safe too. 'And it will give me time to learn the spell,' he thought.

The cloud swirled and eddied around them as they went forward, running again, across the caravan site. It thickened as they climbed the stile. Simon tried to peer through it. If the man was using the cloud to hide himself, he would probably be where it was at its thickest. 'Hurry!' he said, and stood aside as Cafall leapt over the high step after him.

The lane here was like a smoke-filled tunnel. They groped their way along it to the narrow valley.

'We mustn't miss the valley,' Fred said anxiously. 'Keep your eyes peeled, everybody. The path's over-grown with ferns.'

Bethan was in front. She called out: 'Here it is!' and darted forward. Then, suddenly, she stopped. 'I can't go in there,' she said, and now she was really terrified.

Fred peered over her shoulder. Simon heard her moan, but she didn't say anything. She simply stood still and stared along the path. Simon moved up beside her and stared too.

Cloud filled the valley. Cloud that seemed to have substance. Cloud with flesh like thick, ever-moving jelly. Shapes formed. Strange moving shapes. Nothing was real. Nothing was familiar. Trees, ferns, rocks, the cloud itself . . . everything . . . warped and shifted as they stood there looking.

'I can't go in there,' Bethan said again. She blocked the path.

'We've got to. Go on! We can't stay here. Move!'
Fred was trying not to scream at her.

Simon had to do something. He pushed past them.
'I . . . I think it might be better if I go in front with
the horn,' he said. 'If I hold it out, the horn will sort
of lead us, won't it. I . . . I think those shapes can't
be real. It's all put there like this to scare us, to stop
us getting to Miss Emmanuel. Well, we mustn't let it
stop us.'

He sounded brave, but he didn't feel it. He moved
on to the path, hesitating a little. Then he held up the
horn, like a banner, and stepped forward. And as he
took the first step, he felt someone at his side.

It was Cafall. Cafall the warrior. Cafall the leader's
dog. Cafall was at *his* side, helping him. In spite of his
fear, Simon felt a great thrill of joy and pride. For this
moment, Cafall, the great Cafall, was his.

He walked steadily into the valley, and, as he
advanced, the illusion shifted. Each shape dissolved
into the general greyness or melted back into itself,
and the cloud could only wreathe menacingly
around them. It didn't touch them. They passed
straight through it, and, at last, there was Miss
Emmanuel's gate and the chance of safety for a
while.

But they couldn't open the gate. The golden
column of bees stood in front of them. Through it
they heard the old woman shriek. 'Go away, Corn

Du! Go away! Take that Twm with you. Take him
away from here. I know all about him. I don't want
him here. Go away!'

Simon wasn't surprised. He had known that something like this could happen. Fred and Bethan
hadn't. They couldn't believe it.

'She can't do this,' Bethan said, and began to sob.

Fred was now in full panic. 'Shift the bees, Jonesy!

Do something with the horn. Make them move. Fight them! For goodness sake fight them,' she screamed at him.

'I can't . . .' Simon remembered the lightning of the horn. 'I can't. I'd kill them. I can't do that. I'll try to talk to her,' he said.

But there was no time to talk. Even as he called: 'Miss Emmanuel!' Cafall began to growl. Simon whirled around. Behind them, in the undulating cloud, stood a black shape which did not move or change. Twm Cymylau laughed in triumph. They were trapped.

13
Simon Decides to Stand and Fight

It was the bees who saved them. Without warning, they sprang as one cat-like animal leaping at its prey. Twm Cymylau screamed, a terrible, terrifying scream. He turned and ran, his gown not black now, but golden as the insects covered him. Simon felt ill.

'They've all gone, him and them,' Bethan said. 'Let's get in, quick.'

But they still couldn't get into Miss Emmanuel's garden. More bees had come to take the place of those which had gone. Already a thin column stood in front of the gate, and, as they watched, a stream of them, like golden smoke, came swarming from one of the hives.

'It was her they were saving really, not us, wasn't it?' Fred said. 'And she still won't have us here. She's not the sort of friend I'd like to have, Jonesy.'

'She's not a friend,' Simon said bitterly.

'No, she's not, is she.' Fred looked at him seriously. 'You were afraid she would be like this, weren't you?'

'I knew she would be,' Simon said quietly. 'She said she was too old to help.'

'Too old and too nasty,' Fred said. She was still looking serious. '*You* are going to have to be a bit nastier, you know that, don't you.'

'I can't.' Simon felt helpless again. 'I can't be cruel I won't be.'

'I don't mean cruel,' Fred said.

'Miss Emmanuel does when she says nasty. She says I've got to be like her . . . and everybody else who does things like we do.'

'Twm's certainly cruel, isn't he. You can see it. I wouldn't want you to look like him, or *be* like him. *I* don't mean cruel when I say nasty.'

'What do you mean then?' Simon asked miserably. 'Braver, I suppose.'

'No! Certainly not!' Fred said. 'You are brave.' She looked embarrassed. 'At least. *I* think you are. What I mean is, well, that you should be a bit more tough.'

96

'*I* think we ought to run away again.' Bethan was looking anxiously at the cloud. 'Twm won't mind killing them bees, will he, and when he has he'll come straight back at us, won't he.' Bethan wiped her eyes on the sleeve of her shirt.

Simon stood and looked at the cloud. It was whirling now, patchily. It reminded him of leaves in autumn, swirling as a fitful breeze caught them up, played with them, then dropped them again. Occasionally it rippled, too, like a pool when something dropped into it disturbs its surface. The cloud was out of control. Twm had lost his grip on it—for the moment. 'So he's not *that* marvellous,' Simon thought. 'If this cloud is like a blanket of mist while he leaves it to behave naturally,' he said slowly, 'it's going to fill all the hollow places and lie on the lowest ground. And that means that we should be able to get out of it most quickly if we climb up, out of the valley, shouldn't we?'

'Yes!' Fred was instantly ready to lead them. 'There's no footpath on top, but I'll be able to find the way.'

'The way to where?' Bethan asked.

'To anywhere Jonesy decides we should go,' Fred said. 'Come on!'

She wasn't rushing him any more. She was going to give him a chance to think. 'Good old Fred!' Simon thought. 'She's a real friend. And she's helping, *really*

97

helping.' He watched her climbing steadily and sensibly. She wasn't panicking any more. She was picking a safe path, skirting the outcrops of rock, finding footholds in tree roots and among the ferns. Bethan was scrambling after her.

Simon went more slowly. He had to be careful not to drop the horn. He noticed that Cafall, who was bounding from one precarious ledge to another, kept waiting for him. Cafall was still his. 'Cafall's a friend too,' he thought, 'and to think, all I wanted to do was get rid of him.' He realized, suddenly, that he wasn't feeling helpless any more. 'And all because of Fred and Cafall,' he thought.

Fred was jubilant when they reached the top. 'You were right!' She was smiling. 'Jonesy, you were right. Look, there's blue sky above us again. I've never loved blue sky so much . . . and just look at the cloud! Just look at it!'

They stood still, breathing deeply after the climb, and looked down at the top of the cloud.

'It's like rock!' Bethan sounded as though she couldn't believe it. 'It couldn't *be* rock, could it?'

'Of course not,' Fred said. 'We were in it, weren't we? You can't walk around in rock. Brass bedknobs! Do you know what it reminds me of? Pictures of the moon's surface, but with the tops of trees growing out of it. How did Twm make it like that, Jonesy?'

'I don't know,' Simon said. 'It must be something

he's learnt, something he's found out how to do. It must be really powerful magic.'

'Yes, really powerful magic,' Fred echoed him. She sounded uneasy again. 'How are you going to get rid of him?' she asked quietly.

Simon looked across the top of the cloud at the carn. It stood in sunlight, like an island oasis rising in the distance on the far side of a desert. It was good to be able to see it again. But could he reach it? He told Fred and Bethan what he had been thinking, about waiting at the carn, and then getting Cafall to chase Twm Cymylau back into Annwn. 'It's not a good idea, I know,' he said, 'but I can't think of anything else that I can do—unless I wait there for him and then try to make him go back through myself.'

'Fight him, do you mean?' Bethan asked.

'Yes, with the horn,' Simon said. 'The black horn against his wand. I think the horn is more powerful than his wand—at least, it would be if I did the right thing with it.'

'We'd have to hope you were lucky enough to do the right thing, then, wouldn't we?' Fred said.

'Yes.' Simon didn't like to think of relying on luck.

'What makes you think he would turn up at the carn?' Bethan asked.

'He'll find me wherever I go,' Simon said. 'He's found me easily enough so far, hasn't he. I think he always will.'

Fred looked worried again. 'We can't go all that way back to the carn,' she said. 'It's right on the other side of his cloud—and when he gets rid of the bees he's going to be right back in there, isn't he.'

'Where else can I go?' Simon asked. 'The wishing well is right in the middle of the cloud, and so is the churchyard.'

'We can't go back in it,' Bethan said. She had been watching the cloud carefully again. 'Look! It's changing. It's sort of smoothing out and holding still now.'

'It's not!' Fred pointed. 'Look! It's blowing up.'

They all looked to where she pointed. Away on the far side of the cloud, the surface suddenly rushed upwards. A billow of cloud, like smoke exploding from the cone of a volcano, shot towards the sky, then cascaded back on to the dark, smooth, surface, like a black fountain filled with sparkling, golden tinsel dust.

'Golden bees,' Fred said. 'What did I tell you? Twm's killed them. Now he's free. Now he'll come after you again. Jonesy, where can we go?'

Simon stood still, gripping the horn, and gazing at the carn. He could see it so clearly with the horn in his hands. He felt that he had only to reach out and he would touch it. But it was far away and out of reach. He would have to think of somewhere else. He turned his back on it.

It was then that he saw Tŷ Corn Du. He didn't see

the house. He saw the avenue. He saw a blur of green and bronze like a light reflected on the sky. But Tŷ Corn Du was beyond the crest of the hill. It should be hidden by trees and hedges, by the Earth itself.

It was the magic of Tŷ Corn Du that he could see. He could see it, just as he could see the carn, because he was holding the black horn in his hands. And as soon as he saw it he knew what to do. He would go to Tŷ Corn Du, the place which, like his mountain, lived and breathed magic. Yes, he would stand and fight at Tŷ Corn Du.

14

The Way to Annwn

Bethan insisted that they must call Gareth again before they left the top of the valley. 'He might never have left the lane,' she said. 'We might have just missed him somewhere. Gareth, Gareth,' she called.

'Gareth, Gareth,' Simon called too, and his voice seemed to echo back from the carn, far away. But Gareth didn't answer.

They were too tired to run. Fred led them across the fields to a lane which led past a farm where rooks flew up as soon as they came near, and a dog came out to bark at them. Simon laid the horn across Cafall's neck, and Cafall stayed close to him.

Fred knew the farm dog. 'Meg!' she called. 'What's all the fuss about?' She bent and stroked her. 'It must be about tea time,' she said. 'Her people seem to be back from school, judging by the light in their kitchen.'

'Tea time,' Bethan said, she was still holding Gareth's satchel. 'And Gareth never had his dinner. He must be feeling awful hungry.'

Fred tried to cheer her up. 'I know,' she said. 'We'll all go in to my place for tea. What do you think, Jonesy? Could we go in for tea? I know you're supposed to be keeping this all secret, but Meryl would be all right, you could tell her. And she could go and look for Gareth, perhaps. What do you think?'

Simon considered it. It would be quite safe to trust Fred's Aunt Meryl, he was sure of that, and it would be good for Fred to go in for a while, and good for Bethan to think that someone was looking for Gareth, though he was fairly certain that Meryl wouldn't find him. 'All right,' he said, 'we'll go in and ask Meryl what she thinks about it. But we'll have to be quick.'

The avenue stood calm and golden with September sunshine. They trudged along it wearily. Simon was glad that at last they would have somewhere safe to rest. 'I'll have to keep watch to make sure I'm ready when Twm Cymylau comes,' he thought, 'but I'll leave Fred and Bethan inside. I'll come out again as soon as I've learnt the spell. That shouldn't take long.' He began to feel that the terrible nightmare might soon have gone away for ever, that he would win, that he could stop worrying.

But, when Tŷ Corn Du came into sight at the end of the avenue, they saw at once that they couldn't go inside. Parked on the gravel at the front of the house were not only Fred's Uncle Smithy's van and Guy's Morgan, but three other cars too—Mrs Rhys's, Simon's father's and Miriam's.

'Miriam . . . and Mam!' Bethan stood still. 'Miriam's here before us.'

'They all are,' Fred looked dismayed.

'Miriam's followed us. She's a jump ahead of us.' Bethan sounded as though she was going to be hysterical. 'She *is* a witch. She is! Just like Old Blod . . .'

Fred looked upset. 'She's not like her. I'm sure she's not. I liked her. Oh Jonesy, we can't go in now, can we?'

Simon began to worry again. 'No, we can't go in now,' he said.

They stood out of sight among the rhododendrons while Simon decided what to do. 'I was going to tell you two to stay inside the house,' he told them, 'but now you'll have to hide out here. Perhaps you might be safe in the summer house.'

'I'm staying beside you,' Fred said. 'What if he sneaked up the back way across the fields and got at us first. No! I'm staying beside you.'

'I'd feel safest by you, too,' Bethan said.

So Simon learnt the spell as he stood at the corner of Tŷ Corn Du, out of sight of the front door, where he could hide among the rhododendrons quickly if he needed to. He could see the drive from there—he could also see the mountain. He made Bethan and Fred crouch beneath the bushes. Cafall lay at his feet. And they waited.

They waited. And they waited . . . But Twm Cymylau didn't come. Nothing moved in the avenue. There was no breeze, no sound, nothing. The garden of Tŷ Corn Du lay still and silent. Once, Fred and Bethan whispered to Simon. 'Why doesn't he come! I wish he would come.' And the whisper seemed to echo like a shout from the grey, stone walls. Soon afterwards Guy came out and stood on the slate step and called: 'Fred, Fred!' and stood listening, before he went back in.

And when Guy had gone the garden and the avenue were even more quiet than before. Not one leaf quivered in the tall trees. Not one trace of a shiver was there among the tall, dry grasses . . .

And then, without warning, night rushed in to Tŷ

104

Corn Du. Night . . . and the cloud. Like a thick blanket of grey shadow the cloud came unrolling and unfolding. Down it fell upon them, and they were smothered and wrapped in its wet, cold darkness.

Simon was glad to feel Cafall at his feet. Never had he felt so frightened. He stood quite still, trying desperately not to look as though he couldn't see a thing. 'Where is he?' he thought. 'Where is he? I must see him before he sees me or I won't stand a chance.'

But, when Simon did see Twm standing half hidden by the cloud, it was obvious that Twm had already seen *him* long before, and had been waiting, watching him.

Simon looked at him warily . . . and, suddenly, something about the way he was standing, half turned away from him, made him wonder if, perhaps, Twm was worried. The relief, the one, faint hope, made him almost excited. 'Of course!' he thought. 'He's like Miss Emmanuel. He wants to have a look at me. I've got the black horn. I'm Y Corn Du . . . He's not sure about me. He doesn't know if I'm any good or not. He doesn't know if he dares take me on. I've got a chance!'

Carefully, he moved around the corner of the house until he had his back to the front wall of Tŷ Corn Du. He groped behind him until he felt the

105

rough stones against his hand. He wanted to feel the house. Yes, he was there. He was safe against it. He stood quite still. Then, swiftly, he raised the black horn, copying the movement Twm had made with his wand . . .

Lightning split the cloud, and there before him was the mountain, bathed in sunlight. He could have sung. 'The spell!' he thought. 'Now I can chant that spell!'

But, before Simon had even begun the spell, he felt the wall of Tŷ Corn Du begin to move. He didn't turn around. He didn't dare. He had to watch Twm. He had to watch him constantly. He pressed more heavily upon the wall, and felt the stones swing sideways beneath his hand. Still, he watched Twm, and as he watched, suddenly, without even beginning to fight, Twm surrendered. Simon saw his head bow, and the wand fall from his hand as his arms unfolded and hung, helplessly, at his sides. *Then* Simon could turn around.

In front of him lay a hall, dimly lit by burning torches and a fire that blazed in a cave-like open hearth. Above the fire a large animal hung roasting on a spit. Simon could smell the smeech of the fat that dripped from it, burning on the flames.

Beside the fire, a rough, dirty-looking man sat hunched miserably on a settle, drinking from a big, gem-encrusted goblet. At his side a sword gleamed through the cracks of a well-used scabbard. More men sat quietly among the rushes on the floor in the shadows behind him. And on the other side of the hearth sat another man, a clean-shaven, fine-featured man with white hair and sunburnt skin, and strong, long-fingered hands.

Simon noticed the hands just before he noticed the black horn . . . He stood amazed, tightening his grip on the black horn in his world, as he looked at the same black horn hanging on the wall above that enormous fire in Annwn.

Then he looked at the white-haired man, and he saw that the man was now looking at him. The man had the darkest eyes that Simon had ever seen. They were wonderful eyes, full of strength and wisdom, and wonder too, as he noticed the black horn in Simon's hands and glanced up quickly to see that it still hung safely on his wall.

Next moment, there came a distraction—Cafall. Simon hadn't noticed him get up and stand there, gazing suspiciously. Now, suddenly, he roared a sound of recogniton, and with one joyful bound he leapt into the hall. The rough man turned abruptly, and the look of melancholy on his face changed to one of almost disbelieving happiness.

'Cafall!' he called, and leapt to meet the great hound halfway across the floor.

Then, as they roared and wrestled together, one laughing, one growling, both full of joy, the man whom Simon knew must be the First Wizard of Tŷ Corn Du, stooped and picked up a bundle wrapped in a cloak, that lay in front of the fire. He made his way past Cafall and his master and stepped from Annwn into this world.

Simon pressed against the wall. He must hold it open for him. He knew that this man wouldn't want to stay in this world any more than he would want to go through into Annwn. He watched him as he laid the bundle carefully on the grass at his feet and then stood up and stared around him, fascinated by the new Tŷ Corn Du. Simon could see that he liked the avenue, and he was happy when he saw that the mountain was the same as ever. But then he noticed Twm Cymylau, and his whole face changed.

His frown was terrible. Simon saw Twm cringe as the wizard spoke sternly to him, pointing back into the hall, and, as he slunk through back into Annwn, the wizard strode forward, picked up the wand and snapped it in two. He pointed at the cloud, and it whitened with a flash of pure light, soaring away, high up into the sky, where a wind from the mountain caught it and tore it into shreds.

Then the wizard walked back to Simon and stood looking down at him. He asked him something, but Simon couldn't understand. He shook his head.

'Our languages are different,' he told him, and the wizard nodded as though he understood. He glanced over his shoulder and took one more look at the trees and the flowers in the garden before stepping back to where he belonged. Then he smiled gravely at Simon and made a deep bow. And then he told Simon his name. 'Meredith . . . Corn Du,' he said courteously.

Simon smiled happily. 'Meredith! He's got his own name as well as Corn Du . . . So I can have mine too!' He bowed his head politely. 'Jones,' he said. 'My name is Jones . . . Jones of the Black Horn.'

Then Meredith snapped his fingers at Simon and pointed at his hand, and Simon felt his grasp of the wall slip away from him. Next moment the path into Annwn had gone, the strong, safe wall of Tŷ Corn Du stood beside him, and all around was sunshine.

15
Wizard and Witch

It wasn't until the way to Annwn had disappeared that Simon realized that Fred and Bethan had crept out from beneath the bushes and had been standing beside him watching everything. Now Bethan bent down to look at the bundle that the wizard had laid at his feet, and Fred ran up to the front door of Tŷ Corn Du, and pushed it open.

Fred looked as though she was half afraid of what she might see, but Simon saw her relax as she stepped inside. 'It's all right,' she said. 'It's still the same.'

As she spoke, the door from the kitchen burst open, and a flood of parents poured out amid a babble of questions and accusations.

'Oh Simon, why didn't you say anything?' That was Simon's mother.

'You know we would have helped you, surely you do,' his father said.

'I couldn't believe it when they all said it must be true.' That was Mrs Rhys.

'You took the horn so we knew something important must have come up,' Fred's Aunt Meryl said, and Fred's uncle Mr Smith, looked at Simon, as inscrutable as ever, and smiled.

Fred pushed her way through them all to Miriam, who was standing beside Guy. 'You're a friend of Guy's. I can see you are,' Fred said. 'I knew you were nice. I knew there must be some reason why you knew all about Jonesy and me.'

Miriam smiled shyly. 'I thought of trying to explain, but . . .'

A voice interrupted them all, shouting above the general din. It was Gareth. 'Mam! I've been with

Arthur . . . King Arthur!' They all stopped talking, instantly, and stood looking at him. '. . . only he never looked like a king,' he said. 'He was scruffy . . . and Excalibur was tatty.'

Bethan was holding him tightly with one hand. Over her other arm she held the cloak that he had been wrapped in. She was crying with relief. 'It was only the scabbard that was tatty, silly,' she said, shaking him gently. '*Arthur* was wonderful.' She looked at her mother. 'Arthur looked after our Gareth, Mam. He took care of him till Simon beat Twm Cymylau and got him back here again.'

'Yes! Jonesy stood up to Twm Cymylau, *and* got Gareth back from Annwn.' Fred was delighted with it all. 'He got into Annwn just with his hands, you know,' she told everyone. 'He didn't need the spell like Miss Emmanuel was sure he would. He didn't need anything but his hands.'

The questions began to flow. 'How . . .? What . . .? Where . . .? When . . .?' Simon saw that Dr Gimlett was there too, still eager to join in. And suddenly he couldn't bear it. He noticed Mr Smith had made his way across the hall to stand beside him. Mr Smith was watching him. Mr Smith always understood how he felt.

Simon whispered to him. 'Do you think it would be all right if I slipped away? I don't want to upset Mother, but . . . well, I've had enough.'

'I will explain,' Mr Smith said. 'But where will you be? I must tell them where to find you later.'

Simon hadn't thought of where he would go until Mr Smith asked him. Now he realized that he wanted to go home, to go back to the mountain, to make sure that, like Tŷ Corn Du, the mountain and the carn were just the same. 'I'll be at the carn,' he said, then, quickly, he walked away.

He looked across at the mountain as he trod down from the doorstep of Tŷ Corn Du. He still had the black horn. He could still see every grey rock of the carn. 'I'll soon be there,' he said. 'I'll take Fred's short cut . . . And it will be the same. I know it will.'

A golden bee darted from nowhere. He smelt the sweet honey scent and saw its wings like rainbows in the sunlight. Away down the avenue it sped . . . and another one came to take its place.

Simon stood still. In the distance, at the end of the avenue, he saw a gleam of gold. 'The column!' he thought. 'She's sent the column. She's going to make me come to see her again.'

He could hardly believe it. 'Why? She doesn't need me to tell her what happened. She will know that already. She's had them spying on me all the time. So why?'

He walked slowly towards the distant swarm. He would make them wait for him. He was annoyed. He wanted to go home. She had no need to send them like this. But she must have a reason. So, what could it be?

It seemed to Simon as he walked along the avenue that, one by one, every single bee detached itself from the column and flew to have a look at him. And, as he watched them hovering inquisitively over his hands, and buzzing carefully close to his face, he guessed why Miss Emmanuel wanted to see him.

'They've told her that I've changed a bit,' he thought. 'I have too, I suppose. She said that I needed to strengthen and shape up, and I did, today . . . already . . . And they've told her, and now she wants to *see* for herself. Right! I'll go and show her.'

He walked straight up to the golden column and stood in front of it. Then he pointed the black horn right at its heart. 'Go home!' he told it. 'Go on! Go and tell your queen that I'm on my way. I'll come to see her . . . but I won't be driven.' He stepped towards it and the whole column writhed away from him with a noise that sounded like a frightened growl. It vanished. Not one bee was left.

Simon met it again when he reached Miss Emmanuel's gate. It stood on guard, just as it had before. He pointed the black horn at it again, and this time it scattered.

As he walked along the winding path, he heard Miss Emmanuel shrieking at him from inside the cottage. 'Go away! Go away! I'll not let you in.'

'But you sent for me,' Simon said firmly. 'You sent an army to fetch me . . . So I'm coming in.' He laid his left hand upon the door. He felt it shudder as the bolt slid back. He pressed gently. The door swung open.

Down into the beautiful room he stepped, and walked straight up to the fire. Now, he could look at it. The flames no longer hurt his eyes.

Bees dashed around him in confusion, and Miss Emmanuel looked terrified. Simon felt sorry for her, as he stood there, watching her trembling. 'How awful,' he thought. 'How awful to get nothing but fear from something as wonderful as magic.' He tried to smile at her, but he didn't feel like smiling. 'You needn't be frightened of me,' he told her sadly. 'I won't hurt you . . . ever. I'm not nasty, am I? You told me that yourself. And now we both know that I don't have to be. You know what the First Wizard was like now. I'm sure the bees must have told you about him. Well, I'm going to try to be like him.'

'You will be, too. You will be . . . I could see it,' she said, and her voice was shaking. 'I could see that yesterday . . .'

'And now you can see that I'm on the way already,' Simon said. 'I thought I must be.' He took a deep breath. 'Now, before I go home, I've one thing I want to ask you. I want to ask you not to send your bees to spy on me again, please. I don't like it. I'd like you to keep them off the mountain, if you don't mind.'

'But I won't know what's going on,' she whined.

'I'll come and tell you if anything's going on,' he said.

Miss Emmanuel looked at him craftily. 'Regular?' she asked. 'Will you come regular?'

Simon hadn't expected this. He had expected that she would say that she wanted him to keep away from her valley if she kept away from his mountain. 'Why?' he asked suspiciously.

Miss Emmanuel scowled at him. 'Because nobody never comes,' she said. 'It's no visitors I get, never.'

Simon just stood and looked at her. He had planned that this would be the last time he ever saw Miss Emmanuel, but he couldn't be unkind to her. So, knowing that from now on he could expect a regular session of complaints and, no doubt, ridicule, he promised to visit her. 'All right,' he said. 'I'll come to see you regularly.'

'How regular?'

'Once a month. On the last day of every month.'

She was satisfied with that, but only for a moment. Almost immediately she began to look cunning again. 'But what if I should *need* you, Corn Du? Have to send for you then, wouldn't I.'

'All right, if you need me between visits, you can send for me . . . but not the whole army. And I think perhaps we had better agree how many you will send. If you only send one I'll probably think you're spying on me again. Yes, you'd better send a definite number.'

'How many?' she asked.

'How many would you like?'

'Seven!' she snapped.

It was a magic number. Simon wasn't surprised. 'All right, seven . . . or none at all,' he said.

He walked back to the door, then turned and faced her again. 'Goodbye until the thirtieth, then, Miss Emmanuel,' he said politely. Then he remembered something else that he had meant to make clear to her. 'And by the way, my name is still Jones. Please remember, won't you,' he said, and then he left her, shutting the door gently behind him.

16

The Homework Begins

Next morning Fred, Bethan and Gareth all came to Simon's house. Fred came first. She looked rather bewildered, but very happy, as she sat on the steps in the rockery, hugging Bedwyr. 'Jonesy,' she said, 'every time you use the black horn, something as good as magic happens for me.'

'What do you mean?' Simon asked.

'Well, last time I got Smithy for an uncle, and you know as well as I do that he's the most marvellous uncle in the world. Now, this time—I can hardly believe it's true yet—this time I'm getting a mother. Miriam's going to be my new mother. It's what's been the matter with Guy all week. He came down here especially to tell me about her, but couldn't. He was afraid I'd be upset, you see, after the other one being so beastly. He had a right old panic, I can tell you, Jonesy. Miriam told me all about it. He even made her promise to stay hidden in the caravan site in case I should meet her around somewhere before he had introduced us. That's why she ducked out of sight every time we came near. That's why she was miserable, too. She's a very friendly person, a *bit* shy, I think, but, oh, *really friendly*, and she was *longing* to come out and chat to me. She *knew* we'd like each other. She *knew* I wouldn't be upset, and, honestly, I ask you, who could be upset by Miriam? I liked her the moment I met her. Didn't I tell you I did?'

Bethan and Gareth arrived just in time for them to hear Fred's news too. 'So she wasn't a witch,' Fred told Bethan in an 'I told you so' voice.

Bethan shook her head in disbelief. 'I was sure she was,' she said. 'The more I thought about her the more I was sure that she wasn't *ordinary*.'

'Well, actually, you're right. She's not ordinary,' Fred said. 'Do you know what she's crazy about? . . .

Trains! She's got a fantastic model railway, and if she can get Guy to come and live down here instead of in London, she's going to set it up in the attic.'

'Do you think she'd get him to?' Gareth was suddenly interested.

'Yes!' Fred hugged Bedwyr in her delight. 'I think she will, and we can all go up and watch the trains any time we like. She said so!'

Gareth would have asked questions about Miriam's model trains all day, but Simon wanted him to talk about Annwn.

'He can't remember it properly,' Bethan said. 'Can you, Gar?'

'No.' Gareth shook his head. His small, pale face suddenly seemed to be made of very little else but two large, brown eyes. 'I dreamed it, really,' he said. 'Didn't I?'

'No you never!' Bethan sounded exasperated. 'Tell Simon what you remember now, and be sensible.'

Gareth slid along the step until he was sitting close to Simon. The black horn lay between them. He reached out and touched it gently with one finger, then grinned at Simon shyly. 'Dr Gimlett was saying the spell,' he said. 'That's how it began. I know that because I was awake for that bit, but then I thought I went to sleep and dreamed about a lovely place full of apple trees, and it was evening. And this man came looking for his dog what he had lost, and I said:

120

"You're Arthur, aren't you," but he didn't understand me in English so I tried him in Welsh, and then we had a chat. And I said: "Bethan's got Cafall out of Annwn", and he said: "Has she, by Jupiter! We'll have to get Corn Du on to this." And I said: "He's on it already." And then he wanted to know about you, and after I'd told him he wrapped me up in his cloak and carried me up to Tŷ Corn Du in front of him on his horse . . . It was a black one. And he told the real-looking wizard there about you, and they were just wondering what to do about it all when his army came in . . . It was a very little army. And they'd got a pig. They'd pinched it! And I was going to have pork for supper . . . crackling too . . . but then I woke up on the grass outside Fred's house.'

'Still wrapped up in Arthur's cloak,' Bethan said. 'And that proves you never dreamt it.'

'Have you still got the cloak?' Simon asked.

'Yes, we're going to keep it in Tad's mam's oak chest,' Bethan said, 'only . . . it's not going to last . . . the cloak, you know. Sometimes when I look at it it looks just like a shadow, and I know one day I'll lift the lid and it will be faded right away.'

Fred sounded sad. 'That's a shame,' she said. 'It would be nice to have a souvenir. I've got the spell, still, if you want to have that.'

'No!' Bethan shook her head emphatically. 'I do not! You can keep that, Fred, thank you very much.'

121

'Thanks!' Fred laughed. 'I won't use it, ever, but I would like to keep it.' She looked at Simon. 'And what about the black horn, Jonesy? You'll keep it now, won't you?'

Simon smiled. 'Yes, I'll keep it. You were right. It's mine. I ought to have it here, ready to use whenever I need to. I'm not going to be caught out like this again.'

Fred had a far-away look in her eyes. 'You said you needed help, right from the beginning, and you found it. But who would have thought it would be The First Wizard who helped you.' She looked at Simon seriously. 'He was tough, wasn't he.'

Simon thought of the stern, wise face. 'Yes, he was tough,' he said. 'And he knew a lot of magic.'

'He had magic hands, just like yours,' Fred said.

'And you'll be just like him, Simon,' Bethan said. 'I know you will.'

'I think I could be if I can manage to learn a lot of magic,' Simon said.

'How will you do that?' Bethan asked.

'Homework!' Fred said. 'Jonesy's a homework fanatic . . . and I'll bet he's begun it already.'

'Well, actually, I have,' Simon said. 'The words in the first part of the spell were so interesting. I just had to look them up.'

'What did they mean?'

'They're all names . . . names of planets and stars

in the constellation called Aquarius ... And all mixed up with fortune telling and magic making.'

Gareth was running his finger along the spiral of the horn. 'Y Corn Du,' he said dreamily ... Then, 'Jones the Black Horn?' he asked. 'How will you know when you're as good as Meredith Corn Du?'

'That's easy!' Fred answered for Simon. 'Jones of the Black Horn will be as good as Meredith Y Corn Du, when he can shut the doorway to Annwn with just one snap of his fingers.'

Simon laid his hand upon the black horn and looked up at the carn high above him. He smiled, happily. 'You always seem to get things right, Fred,' he said, 'and this time I hope ... no, I'm not just going to hope. This time I'm going to make sure that you have.'